Wasted in Love

Wasted in Love
by Allan Wilson

CARGO

Cargo Publishing (UK) Ltd
Reg. No. SC376700
www.cargopublishing.com

© 2011 Allan Wilson

"Wasted in Love"
Wilson, Allan
ISBN – 13 978–0–9563083–9–9
BIC Code–
FA Modern and contemporary fiction (post c. 1945)
FYB Short Stories

CIP Record is available from the British Library

Cover designed by Julie Mackay 2011
Typeset in Scotland by Julie Mackay
The moral right of the author has been asserted.
First Published in the UK 2011
Published by Cargo Publishing
Pinted and bound by the CPI in England

Acknowledgement

Grateful acknowledgement is made to
Gutter and East Dunbartonshire Libraries
for publishing stories from this collection.

In memory of Kenneth Robertson (1984 -2005).

For Julie, everything.

Contents

"When love is not madness, it is not love."
Pedro Calderon de la Barca

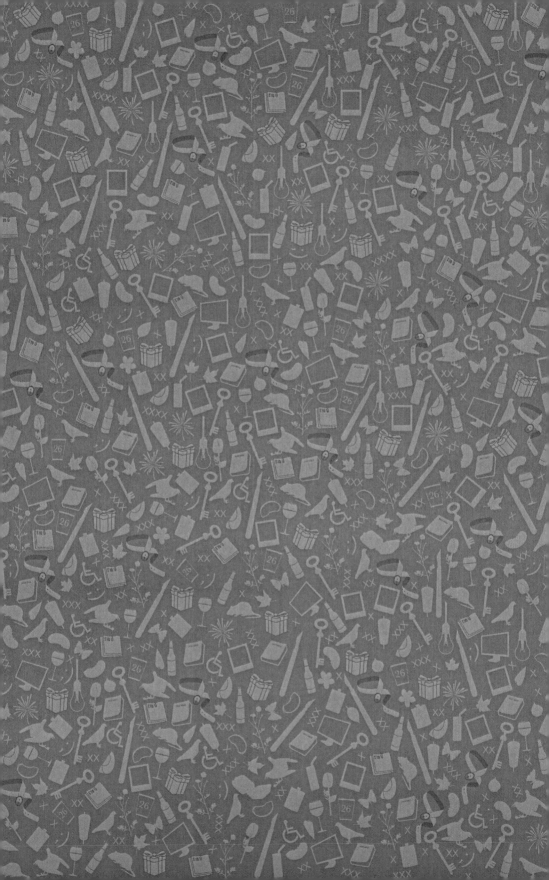

A Celebration

I'm sitting with Jack having a few beers when he eventually gets round to asking. He says, "Tony will you...will you be my best man?" He says it like a proposal.

It's after that the two of us really get to drinking. The girls are out celebrating and me and Jack have all night. He says my sister cried when he asked her. That he was on one knee and she wept. He asks if I ever plan on making an honest woman of Eve.

At one point I suggest we hit the supermarket to get more drinks. But I don't say supermarket, I say supermarché. And I know I'm pretty much gone. That's when Jack tells me to wait a minute. He comes back from the kitchen with the good stuff.

"This is a celebration," he says. "If we're not meant to drink it tonight then we're never meant to drink it."

Later, when the TV goes to static and we've started drinking the whisky slow, Jack tells about when he was a kid and his Mum decided he'd be better off home schooled. "Two months we lasted," he says. "But then my Dad found out and he got the courts involved. The funny thing is I loved school. I only put up with being at home for her." He tells again about the time he met Quentin Tarantino. About how they stood side by side at urinals during the Monte Carlo

Grand Prix. I've heard him tell that one a few times. He always uses the same punch line: "I looked down. Then Tarantino looked down. We made eye contact. I winked. Then Tarantino went pale."

I ask Jack if he's ever heard me tell about the time I got locked in a disabled toilet and had to climb into the ceiling. He's heard it. I ask if I ever told him about my sister's friend I refused to kiss during school who's now a model in Japan. My sister told him that one. I ask if I ever told him Eve's story. About the time someone left a puppy on her doorstep. "Someone's told me," he says. "Maybe it wasn't you but I definitely know that story. How the puppy was just lying at the door wrapped in a blanket then they had that party and the puppy... Yeah, I know all about that one. It's a good one."

"What about the time with the Doctor. Have I ever told you that story?"

"What's this?" he says.

"Man, this is a good one," I say. "If you think the puppy story is a good one, wait until you hear this."

So I start to tell him.

"I was in the pub at the bottom of the road. Normally I go to the shit one 'cause it's quiet and cheap but I'd had a pretty tough week and decided to go to the nice one. You been in?"

"Only with you," Jack says.

"Well anyway, they've split it into two sections so that the restaurant is completely separate from the bar. Means if anyone is eating they don't have to put up with the drinkers. And the drinkers don't have to put up with them. It was about lunchtime I went in. I hurried through the restaurant to the bar. The restaurant was mobbed but when I went through the curtain I was the only person. You can't hear a thing from the other side. It even smells different in there. So I went up to the bar and ordered. I wasted my change on the puggy then grabbed a newspaper.

"A couple of minutes later a guy came in. Well dressed. He had a scarf on. Leather gloves. He went up to the bar and I looked over the top of my paper at him. He ordered a whisky. But then he looked over at me and said to the barman, 'And I'll take a pint of whatever he's having.' I thought to myself here's some old pervert. But fuck it, a drink's a drink, right? Then he went and sat down in the other corner of the room, sipped the whisky then started on the pint.

"The next time I went up to the bar I ordered a pint but then I thought, I know what I'll do, and I said in a pretty loud voice, 'And I'll have a glass of whatever whisky he's having as well.' I said it so loud that the guy looked over. Then I took my drinks, sat back down and slammed the whisky in one.

"After that, if you want to know the truth, I pretty much forgot all about him.

I was getting lost in the papers and with it being so quiet in there I was thinking aye, I could really get used to this place. Maybe it's worth spending that little bit extra for a classy joint like this. I was looking around thinking yeah, even just once a week as a treat I could come here instead of going to the shit pub. Now you've got to remember that I still had enough redundancy cash to last me another three months or so. I wasn't even worrying about that. But then what happened was we synchronised, you know. I'd be at the bar then he'd be at the bar. I'd be at the pisser then he'd walk in. The second time it happened I said something like, 'Fancy meeting you here.' You know, something stupid and the old guy laughed. Then he said, 'Come here often?' And I laughed. But then he said, 'No, I'm asking. Do you come here a lot?' I told him how I normally go to the other pub. 'Is it always this quiet?' I said and he said, 'I don't know. I don't normally drink in the afternoons.' 'Yeah, me neither,' I said, then went like that, whoooooop, with my nose.

"By the time we sat down I'd worked out that this guy was pretty ruined. His eyes were slow and he was shaky on his feet. See, with the black curtain, it's really dark in that section of the place and even though it's lunchtime you always feel like you're one drink away from last orders. So I said to him, 'How come you're in here drinking today then?' and he rubbed his eyes and went, 'I finish up next week. Decided to take a half day. What they going to do? Fire me?' Then he started to laugh. This was the laugh to end them all. More to shut him up than anything else I said, 'So what is it you do then?' When he eventually stopped laughing, he said, 'I'm a surgeon. At least I was. Now I'm a retired surgeon.'

'Surgery?' I said. 'What type of surgery?'

'Breasts mostly,' he said. 'Breast enlargements, breast reductions, breast uplifts, nipple corrections. Nipple tucks. That type of thing.'

'Shut the fuck up,' I said.

'I'm serious,' he said. 'Breasts have been my life work.'

But he was smirking a bit and I said, 'I wish they'd been mine.'

"I started to imagine seeing them cut up so I said, 'Does the novelty not wear off though? Do you not sometimes get sick of tits?'

He sipped the whisky and said, 'Would you?'

I raised my eyebrows.

'Well there's your answer then,' he said.

'And you're retiring man?' I'd work that job to the death.'

We all get old,' he said.

"For a while we chatted about his retirement and I told him what had happened with my job. He said his name was Francis. That his Mother had named him after the Saint. He asked me if my mother had been religious and named me after Saint

Anthony. I said she'd named me after my Dad. He went up and bought us a round
then later I did the same thing. We were just chatting to each other. It was good.
And that laugh. When he got started. How contagious it was. I went up to the
bar to get another round in and the bar tender, he goes like that with his dour
plum-sucking face, 'Yous two are going to have to keep it down or I'll stop serving.'

'Are you kidding on mate?' I said, 'There's nobody here to annoy.'

'Through there,' he said, and pointed his thumb at the curtain.

'Och lighten up man,' I said.

'I'm being serious,' he said, 'I mean it right. I'll stop serving yous. I will,
don't test me. You wanting to test me 'cause you'll see, I'll stop serving. Just you
wait, I'll do it, blah, blah, blah and all that crap.'

"So I took the drinks over and whispered to Francis, 'We've been ordered to
keep it down by the drill sergeant over there.' He looked over at the barman and
said, 'Oh, right. I see.' And for a while we stopped talking. Eventually I got round
to telling him Eve's story. I asked him, 'Do you like dogs Francis?'

'I really like dogs,' he said. 'I love puppies.'

'Aye,' I said, 'I bet you do. In your line of work.'

'Funbags,' he said.

Then that laugh.

"The barman glared over and Francis held his hand up in apology. I ended
up telling him how Eve made these posters describing the puppy. But stupidly,
almost before anything else, she named him. I said how she called him Rory
'cause she thought his growl sounded like a baby lion trying to roar.

'Aww God, the worst thing you want to do is name the damn thing,' the Doctor
said. Then he went, 'I do that with breasts sometimes. You see a lot of women.
Some come in with lopsided ones. Paps with personalities I call them.'

"I ended up telling the guy how she put posters up three miles in every direction.
He was leaning close in and I could smell his breath. I told him how Eve put ads on
the internet, called the local paper. Then I said how that night she had
to go to a party and didn't want to leave the wee guy so she took him with her. I told
him how everyone was fawning over the dog calling Rory, Rory, trying to teach him
paw, trying to teach him fetch but the wee guy just wanted to stay with Eve and curl
up in her chest.

'It's a very nice place to curl up,' the doctor said.

"I explained to him how one thing led to another and Eve ended up drunk.
Rory was fine so she went mingling and eventually met this guy. Now this is a while
before I knew her and I don't mind admitting she ended up sleeping with the guy
but I'm with her now, you know. As long as it was before my time, right?

"I told the Doctor how Eve met this guy. I said, 'I'm sure I don't have to tell you Doc, but when you meet someone new like that and you both get those feelings you forget about everything else, don't you?' I told him how she claims she never forgot Rory, said she was just sure her friends would be looking after him, but for whatever reason she ended up in the bathroom with this guy, his name was fucking Colin or Charles or Clarence or something. Actually, why am I lying, his name was Craig. Just makes me fucking angry to say the guy's name out loud.

"Anyway, one thing led to another and they ended up shagging. So Eve says nowadays that she half remembers hearing scratching at the door. Half remembers hearing Rory's growl. But I said maybe she just thinks that now because of the guilt and she couldn't promise that wasn't the case.

"I was waiting on the doctor hugging me or something. Telling me that Eve was with me now so that other guy didn't matter. That I must be much better if she chose me over him. That she must love me. But he didn't. He just said, 'Can you keep a secret Anthony?'

'Aye,' I said, 'but gonna call me Tony, you're making me feel old.'

'I take photographs,' he said.

'You take photographs?'

'It's standard procedure.'

'What is?' I said.

'No, no, no,' he said, 'in private practices it can be standard procedure.'

'Fucking hell, you mean of the tits?'

'What's not standard practice,' he said, 'is keeping the pictures of the girls that end up going in a different direction. The ones that decide surgery isn't for them or go to a different clinic. But I've not gotten to where I am by following standard procedure.'

'You want to see a few?' The Doctor said.

"Now, you know me. You know how polite I am with strangers. I hate starting new relationships off on the wrong foot. So even though I'm feeling like a duty of care or something for these girls, that I'm worrying about all the times I've ever been to a doctor, about all the times Eve has ever been. I don't say any of this to this Francis guy. I mean, in the back of my head I'm thinking about what doctors must have whispered to each other about her after an examination, but you know how polite I get. Did I tell you about the time I got my haircut by a racist barber? Well yeah, I didn't want to upset him. I just let him carry on.

"We ended out the back of the pub. Lads together and all that. He had his arm around me and we were spilling pints everywhere. The doctor glanced about and when he was sure there was nobody around he opened his jacket and took a couple of Polaroids out his pocket.

'Now these are only the ones I took today,' he said.

"He showed me these photographs of women against a white wall and they were topless. One of the women was covering her eyes with her forearm but the other was just staring straight down the lens.

'She was good,' the doctor said. 'A Mizzzz Symington. Divorced. Very much the entertainer. She wants to enlarge from a 34C to a 34DD.'

"And there was me man, staring at this girl's tits. Unbelievable. Anyway, he went on to tell me how he has a room in his house where he has albums. He said when he first started taking the photographs he would never capture the face. He'd focus purely on the breasts. Nowadays he tries to get in as much of the face and body as he can. He told me I should see the haircuts. That the funniest thing about it all is the change in haircuts. He's got photos going back twenty years, he said, you should see some of the hairstyles, God.

'Do you remember all the women?' I said.

'Only the most recent. The most recent are always the best.'

"We heard the door open and the Doctor stashed the photos back in his pocket.

'Yous are still too noisy,' the barman said. 'It's carrying all the way through to the restaurant. This is the last time I'm warning yous then you'll be out.'

'Our apologies,' Francis said. He smiled at the guy. He had that charming bedside manner, you know. 'My fault,' he said. 'Not the boy's. I'm a retiree. We are having a retirement celebration. But we apologise. The noise will stop.'

'Well okay then. That's good then,' the barman said.

"We sat on the bench beneath the smokers' heater and drank. Every so often I got a fit of the giggles and Francis shrugged or said something like, 'Just one of the perks', or, 'It's a tough job but someone's got to do it'.

"We finished our drinks and I said to him, 'You want another one?' He looked at the glass for a while, checked his watch and said, 'Afraid not young man, I'll have to be going.'

'It's still early man,' I said, 'have another.'

'It's late for me,' he said, 'but have a few more. My treat.' He dipped into his pocket and brought out some cash and handed me it. Thing is, behind the note was one of the Polaroids. The one of the girl with her hand across her face.

'You made this day bearable,' the doctor said.

'Thanks,' I said.

'Enjoy the gift,' he said. 'And listen, don't worry about your girl. Let me tell you, she'll make a great Mother. Keep that in mind. If she did that for a puppy then think what she'd do for a baby.'

And with that the guy was gone.

"I sat for a while and finished the dregs at the bottom of my glass. I was thinking about what he said. And then it started to dawn on me that maybe he was being sarcastic. Maybe he was telling me she'd sleep around. And I couldn't get this thought out of my head. That this Doctor, who has known more women than I'll ever know, he was saying that my girlfriend wants to fuck other guys. I started getting that watery feeling in my mouth, you know, the biley feeling that comes just before sickness, but I managed to calm it down. Instead of buying more drinks I took the guy's money and headed up the road. I stopped in at the Supermarket to buy a bottle of red and a couple of steaks so I could start making us dinner.

"When we were eating I began to tell Eve all about him. But obviously I didn't tell her everything. I just told her what he told me. About what he does.

"And Eve stood up. Said we should call the hospital and tell them. Call the papers, call the police. I told her I didn't even catch his name. That he was probably just a janitor with a wild imagination. But she said, 'No, we have to do something. This is big, it's sick. He's a sick man. What pub was it?' I told her I got the train into town and went to a pub near the station. The guy could be from anywhere.

'I really can't believe this,' she said. 'I feel like I'm going to be sick.'

"Later on, once I'd done the dishes, she was sitting with the laptop.

'This is why you can't trust men,' she said. 'You hear stories like this and you know you can't trust men.'

'You can trust me,' I said.

'I can't trust you. You know fine well I can't trust you.'

'That's not fair,' I said. 'I'm actually fucking raging you're even saying that. That's fucking out of line.'

"Eve walked away and sat in the kitchen. And you want to know what I did? I almost left. I almost went back down to the pub to try and find the guy. For a second I actually missed him."

Jack sits forward and shakes his head.

"Jesus Christ," he says, "what a fucking psycho."

"I know man," I say.

"Look listen," he says, "I was unfaithful once. It was ages ago."

"What?" I say.

"I know, I know, sorry. But you're my best man now. I need to tell you this stuff. It was so long ago, I'm talking years and well, you know how it is."

"But that's my sister, mate."

I'm about to say something else when we hear a key in the door. We hear their voices in the hall and quiet laughter as they tiptoe about so as not to wake us. I hear Eve's whisper and her footsteps pad on the laminate. And all I want is to tell her I'm sorry. That I'll love her forever and I'm sorry.

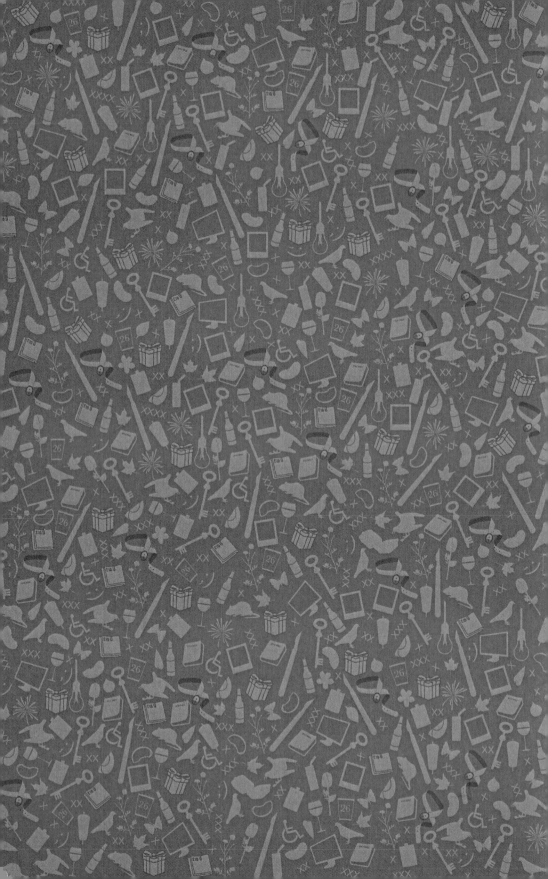

Peaches

I'd dented the hip flask. Below 'Happy 21st' the stainless steel bubbled in.
The contents tasted the same though. An eighteen year old single malt so strong
it made your eyes water. Maybe that was what Ray had liked about it. The first
goes I'd poured into glasses half emptied of water but all it did was prolong the
experience. If you drink it straight, you forget more quickly. 'Happy 21st Alex,'
it said, 'From Ray, Mikey and Steven.' The dent just below the R in Ray.
I'd ruined it. But who else had one from him?

I took two quick swigs then shook the flask. About a quarter left. It fit into
the inside pocket at a push. I got my phone out and typed "I'm in. Come now x."

The question was whether to get ready now or wait for her. It was just a
standard suit I'd bought; single breasted, black. Steven had loaned me a belt for
it because the only ones I had were from school and the leathers were buckled.
They fit though. You can lose a lot of weight in just a week. You get these 1 kilo
tubs in the supermarket. Long life fruit. There must be a hundred peach segments
in there and they float amongst the sap and each other. There were empties piled
up under my bed. It wasn't a breakfast, lunch, dinner type of thing, I'd just graze
on peaches from when I woke up right through to bed time.

Annie came down from Edinburgh most nights. She'd finish up her classes and get the train straight. She said that I should move back in with my Mum for a while. I wanted to stay with the boys. We made a shortlist of twenty songs and sent Ray's Mum the CD, not knowing which ones she would pick. When we were sitting in the funeral aisles and the speakers started playing *This Charming Man* I nearly smiled. Steven was in tears.

Annie would lie beside me and eat the peaches too. I told her that when we were older we should grow our own batch.

"If we still live in Scotland we'll have to buy some sort of special greenhouse to get peaches of this quality. This juicy. To cultivate something like this you need a special greenhouse."

Annie said if that was what I wanted then that was what we'd do.

"Or if we ever manage to escape this fucking country then it won't be as difficult. We can just grow them in the back garden or on the veranda."

Either she'd stay and go home in the morning or she'd get the last train back to Edinburgh. I'd walk her to the station and tell her not to bother coming down the next night, but she always would.

She replied to the text: "Come out. I want to talk to you here. X"

I sent back saying "No. You come in. More private x ;)"

I undid the belt. There was a blue handrail next to the toilet and I folded my trousers over that. I left my phone on the cistern. I put my socks inside my shoes and put them out of the way and under the sink then sat back down on the toilet seat. The plastic stung cold against the back of my thighs. I pressed down on it with my hands and managed to lift my whole body into the air, held up just with my two palms. If I got her kneeling on the seat with her fingers pressed against the wall behind then it would definitely hold her. If I went on my tip toes I'd reach. We could go over to the sink as backup. There was a mirror above it and we'd be able to see each others' face if she bent over and I stood behind her. I'd keep my suit jacket on. It'd be like getting fucked by a Reservoir Dog.

There was a knock on the door.

"Who is it?" I said.

"Is everything okay in there?" a man said.

"Yeah mate, won't be long."

"The emergency button has been pressed. Are you able to release it?"

I looked about. On the wall to my side the red button had been depressed and I pulled it back up.

"That's us now," the guy said.

There was the emergency button then two pull chords; one next to the sink and the other hanging down behind the cistern. I guess they've got a key in case the worst happens.

My phone vibrated.

"Come out please. It's disrespectful to his mum and dad. Xx."

I typed quickly. "You're being horrible to me. Stop being selfish. This is a hard day for me xx"

I stood up and paced the few footsteps to the door and back. There was another mirror on the wall to the side of the door. It was vertical and showed the full height of me. My shirt hung down as far as my thighs and then it was just bare legs and feet. There were goosebumps on my thighs and the soles of my feet were freezing cold against the floor. I walked back to the toilet to get my phone.

"At home we can do whatever you want, but not here. You know it's not right. Xxxx"

I had a swig of the whisky before replying. "You're not fuckin right."

I went over to the full length mirror and started to fondle. The phone vibrated again and I ignored it. I stood side on and stroked. The shirt kept getting in the way so I took the bottom of the button row and stuck it in my mouth. At least I could see everything.

There was a knock on the door. I stared at it for a second then spoke.

"Is that you?"

"Is everything okay in there?" the man said.

"I'll be two fuckin minutes mate."

I waited but there was no reply.

The phone went again.

"I'm so, so, so sorry. Please come out. I love you. Xxxx"

I put the capital letters on and I was typing YOU ARE A FUCKING when it started ringing. It was Steven.

"Alex... You alright?"

"Aye mate, brand new."

My voice echoed around the room.

"I've bought you a whisky. It's sitting here waiting on you."

"Aye."

"Wait two seconds mate..."

I heard Steven saying sorry and excuse me to a few people. There was some laughter, the sound of a party, in the background of the call.

"You still there?" he said.

"Aye."

Steven spoke quickly. "You've nearly got Annie crying out here man. Come out and do this properly."

"Properly?"

"Aye, properly. People are starting to head off and they're asking where you are."

"Say that I'm doing a shite."

"Naw, you're being shite."

"..."

"You coming out?"

"Soon."

"Is it the disabled toilet you're in?"

"..."

"I'm outside it."

There were a few raps on the door.

"Want to let me in?"

I looked down at my bare feet.

"Can you tell Annie to come. I need to talk to her in here."

"Come out here and talk to her."

"I fucking can't. I've got a fucking issue right. It's embarrassing. I need to talk to her in here."

"..."

"..."

"Today isn't about you mate."

"Aw get to fuck man."

I went back to composing the text message to Annie. I deleted the capitals and wrote "Getting Steven to do your fucking dirty work are you?"

I took his belt from the handrail. Although it was leather it even fucking smelled like him. Took on his scent like clothes do. Did he have a hip flask? Did he fuck. Who was he to say where I was? It was hard to get the belt around my arm the way junkies do it. There weren't enough notches for the pin to tighten it around the top. I got it with my teeth and pulled as tight as I could but it kept coming loose and even slapping the back of my forearm didn't raise any veins. I got them jutting out the skin in my wrist by gripping just above it and opening and closing my palm. They say that if you stabbed yourself in the groin with a Stanley knife you'd be dead within the minute. The artery going into my wrist was so fuckin irrelevant. It wasn't much thicker than a vein. I prodded at it. My hand started to tingle. When the phone went with another text I held for a few more seconds then let go.

"Well done mate. She's away to the bathroom crying. Good job."

"Today's not about her ya prick." I replied.

It took a second then the phone started ringing. When I answered I didn't speak.

"Are you there?" Steven said.

"..."

"We've all had a drink mate but it's not an excuse. Stop being selfish. You'll regret it."

"And what?"

"Right listen. You're not gonna be shaggin in that toilet today. She doesn't want to shag you. So come out, have a fuckin drink, say sorry to your bird and sit down."

"..."

"Get out here now."

I hung up then got the hip flask out. Even twisting the cap off in that room seemed loud. It fell to the floor and drove towards where my shoes were. As I drank I put my ear against the wall. Maybe she'd be in there and I'd be able hear her crying. That might be enough.

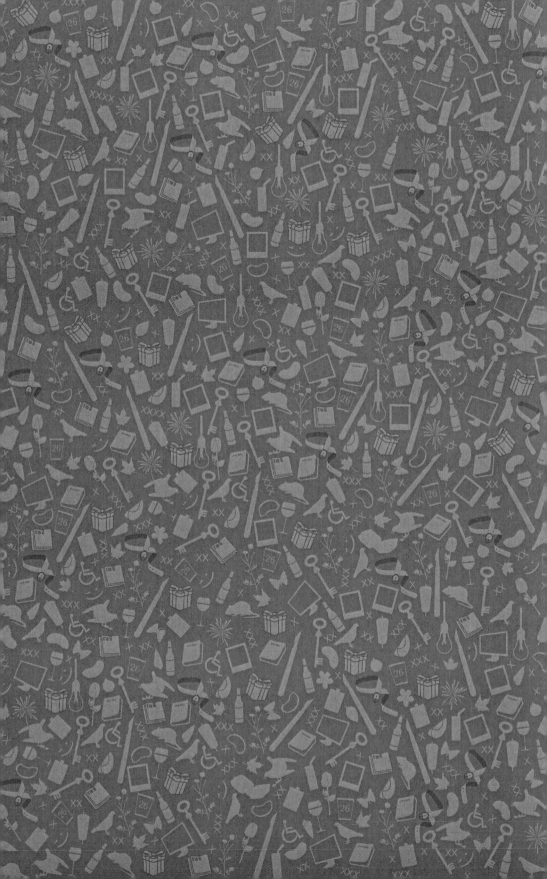

Dangers Far Worse Lost than Run

When the man's hand falls onto Susan's thigh she stays still. She can see parts of him. The black hair falling over his face as his head rests against the window. She looks at the hand on her leg. He has a silver ring on each finger and a star tattooed on the loose skin between his thumb and forefinger. Maybe he's drunk. His fingers twitch on her tights. The hem of her skirt is over his thumb. His hand is warm.

With each jerk the bus makes it could slide off. It could fall onto the seat, into mid air or on to his own thigh. Susan scratches her ear, glancing between strands of his hair at the face. His eyes are open. He lifts his head from the glass and looks at her but the hand does not move. It stays on her thigh like it's a part of her, its softness becoming a hold. The thumb on the front, his pinkie on the softer flesh inside. He sweeps his hair back from his face and she sees him now, fully, for the first time. His rough skin, his jaw tight shut, eyes watching hers. They don't look away from each other. His little finger strokes up and down. The softness of her inside thigh. It could be the jerking of the bus.

She covers his hand with her purse and his grip tightens.

"Next stop," he says, "we can get off at the next stop."

She lets him take her hand as he leads her into the pub. It's busy and they have to walk around twice before finding somewhere to sit. They settle on a circular table in a warm, windowless corner. Their grip on each other is sweaty. They sit on two seats at the wall side of a table, facing out to the crowd. He tells her he'll only be a minute.

When he returns he has a pint of lager, a red wine and what looks like gin and tonic.

"Forgot to ask what you'd want, so..."

He puts the wine and the gin in front of Susan. She lifts the wine to take a drink.

Quickly the man lifts his pint glass to his lips. "Cheers," he says.

Susan takes a long drink of the wine then puts it back down. Her hand shakes as she moves it to her lap.

"Thank you," she says.

The man takes another drink before speaking. "I needed that," he says. Then, "What's your name?"

"Susan. What's yours?"

"Whatever you want it to be." He smiles, coughs. "Naw, it's Marcus but my pals, they call me Colt."

"Colt?"

"Aye, like the gun."

Susan nods, takes another sip of the wine. She looks around the pub. This is Anniesland. It's not too far from her house.

"You can call me Colt," he says.

Susan nods but doesn't meet his eye.

There is a group of men standing in front of them watching the football on the TV above. They are blocking the table and a few others beside it from the rest of the pub.

"Do you have kids Susan?" Colt says.

She laughs at this.

"So you do then," Colt says. "What have you got?"

There is still wine left but Susan reaches for the gin and tonic.

"I've got two little girls," she says. "They're two and three."

She drinks and it steadies her voice.

"What about you, Colt?"

"A wee boy, aye. Don't get to see him much. He lives in Edinburgh with his Mum. He's seven now. No eight. He was eight in April there."

Susan smiles at him.

"Where are your kids now?" he asks. "Is your man watching them?"

"No, we have a childminder. I pick them up after work."

"Aw, I see. Where is it you work?"

"Aw, em... Don't ask. It's one of these jobs where you... Oh forget it, please, you don't want to know. It would bore you, trust me. Just another job."

"Okay, no bother." Colt sips his beer then says, "Where do you live?"

"Live? I live in..."

Susan lifts the gin and takes another drink. She sips the drink slowly and the ice rattles against her teeth. Condensation drips from the glass. She exhales. "It's hotter in here than it was on that bus isn't it?"

"Aye. It's hot alright." He wipes his forehead with the back of his hand. "I stay in Blairdardie. Do you know it?"

"Yes, aye. I know it."

"It's not far. About a fifteen or twenty minute walk."

"Oh right."

"It's a nice night for a walk," he says.

They look at each other. Colt puts his hand on Susan's thigh.

Susan looks about the pub and says, "It would take me about an hour. Look at these heels."

She unwraps her leg from under the table, making Colt move his arm away, and lifts up her foot.

"Four inches. And your feet are meant to swell in warm weather. They've been killing me all day."

"Aye, that's right. Your feet do swell. It's like when you put a bottle of beer in the freezer. More often than not it'll smash. 'Cause of the temperature change."

"Is that right?" Susan says.

"Aye. I've seen it happen."

Colt looks around the pub then has a sip of his beer.

"We'll just leave the walk the now eh? Maybe later though?"

Susan nods and drains the glass of gin. Colt takes a sip of beer then another until all is gone. He raises the glass towards Susan. "Same again?"

"Let me."

Susan brings a twenty pound note out of her purse and hands it to Colt.

"Don't be daft. Put your money away."

"No I insist. You bought the first round, I'll get this one. It's only fair."

"Put your money away. I'm trying to impress you here sweetheart. Did I no tell you I drive a Ferrari? I just get the bus for the banter."

"Come on now, don't make me feel guilty about you buying me all the drinks."

Colt is already walking away. He turns back and smiles at Susan, waving his hand and shooing away her gestures to stretch over with the money. When he is out of reach she puts the note back in her purse. Pictures of her children when they were babies look up at her from the plastic pocket. She zips the purse shut.

He is away a long time. Susan stands up to try and see through the crowd and can just make out Colt standing at the bar and talking to a man. They are laughing. The man is a little younger than Colt, dressed in a similar style: leather jacket and baseball cap. He and Colt lean over and talk into each other's ear when they speak. They laugh together. The man shakes Colt's hand, pats him on the back and hands him something which Colt puts in the inside pocket of his jacket. When he leaves the bar Susan sits down quickly so she can't be seen.

"I just got you the same again," says Colt. "Keep forgetting to ask but I thought you must have liked them."

"No that's fine," says Susan. "Thanks again."

He sips his drink.

"I met an old pal and couldny get away. I'd heard he'd died about a year ago. I thought I was seeing ghosts. Is that one too strong? I think the guy might have made it a double."

Susan takes a drink. Blinks.

"Oh, it is strong. It's fine though. I'll have the wine first anyway."

"You sure?"

"Yes, aye. Thank you."

"Nae bother."

Colt lifts his glass to Susan's. "Cheers," he says, then clinks his glass to hers.

"Cheers Colt."

She feels Colt watching her as they drink.

"So do you know this area?" he says.

"Anniesland? Yeah actually. I lived here for a while. When I was a student, mind you."

"I see, I see. When was that?"

"That'd be telling, wouldn't it."

Colt grins. "I know your age anyway," he says.

"Oh you do, do you?"

He leans in close and says, "Well, maybe not your exact age but a ballpark figure."

"And?" says Susan.

She feels her knee being stroked by his fingers.

He holds his chin and narrows his eyes, looking her up and down.

"I mean the eyes... They're young, very young. And the skin, flawless. But you know the biggest giveaway?"

"Go on then."

"Your body, that's what. The thing is... You're sexy Susan. Do you know how sexy you are?"

Susan feels her cheeks going red. She looks away to the pub and says, "Thanks? Is that what I'm meant to say to that?"

"Say whatever you want. It's the truth."

"Say that to all the girls do you?"

"Are you aware of the effect you're having on every man in here?"

Susan looks at the men transfixed by the TV screen above.

"I wouldn't say that," she says.

Colt looks over and tuts.

"Not the walking dead. I mean anyone with a pulse."

Susan laughs and one of the old men looks over. She raises her hand and says sorry.

"You got a problem pal?" Colt says.

The old man returns his focus to the screen.

"Aye, that's what I thought."

Susan goes quiet and looks down at her lap. On Colt's hand, the veins are blue and bulging through the skin. The way he holds her. She's never seen fingers like his on her body.

"Fuckin dick," Colt says.

They sit in silence for a while. Susan checks her watch.

"Hey," he leans close and grips her arm, "can't let a couple of idiots ruin our day, eh? Maybe get out of here, what you think? Go a wee wander. You could show me some of your old haunts."

"I don't know if I can."

He stares at her.

"I used to come here sometimes though," she says.

"Aye?"

"Looked nothing like it does now."

"I've been coming for years."

"Maybe we've met before then, what do you think Colt?"

"Who knows. It's a small world after all."

They sit quietly for a while. Colt downs what is left of his pint then shakes his head.

"Nah, I'd remember if we'd met. Trust me on that."

He is staring at her.

"What is it?" she says.

"Nothing, nothing. Just thinking how good I've got it."

"Hmm," Susan says.

Colt moves in close and almost whispers.

"I was thinking. I wouldn't mind standing you a taxi if you want to come round and see the flat. There's a rank just across the road."

"I don't know," she says.

"You want to have a couple of more drinks here first?"

"I'd like that."

"You ready for another one then?"

Susan looks at her glass.

"Not yet. I'll get the next one when I'm finished."

There's a commotion quite near them and the smash of a glass. When the barmaid comes over to clean it up Susan is sure she recognises her. She's the girl who babysat a couple of times.

Susan clears her throat but the girl doesn't look over. When the glass has been cleared the girl goes away. Probably wasn't her anyway.

Susan finishes the wine and checks her watch.

"Somewhere you need to be?" says Colt.

"The kids, it's just… You know."

"Can you not just leave them with the babysitter? Call her and tell her the bus blew a gasket or something?"

"Well yes and no. It's just… Look, I shouldn't be here."

Colt laughs at this.

"I'm being serious Colt. Is this something you do all the time?"

"Susie, calm down darlin. Look, sit down, relax, enjoy the drink."

"My name is Susan," she says.

"Okay, okay."

Colt raises his hands in defence.

"Look Susan, I thought we were just having a nice drink here and getting to know each other. Don't worry. I'm just a guy who seen a good looking woman and took a chance. You know? No regrets and all that. But if you want to, go."

"I do yes. I want to go."

"Well feel free."

Susan stands up.

"Thank you for the drink Colt."

"Aye, whatever you want. Maybe see you again."

Outside the air is damp. Clouds hide the sun now and there's a fine rain. Susan leaves the pub and crosses the road to the bus stop where some people huddle under the shelter. She stands amongst them and looks back to the pub. There are smokers chatting and laughing on the steps outside. Maybe there're people about who know her, who know her family. There is no sign of Colt. Susan opens her purse and looks at her phone. She puts it back in her bag. She laughs, loud enough that people turn to look. She shakes her head and stands among them.

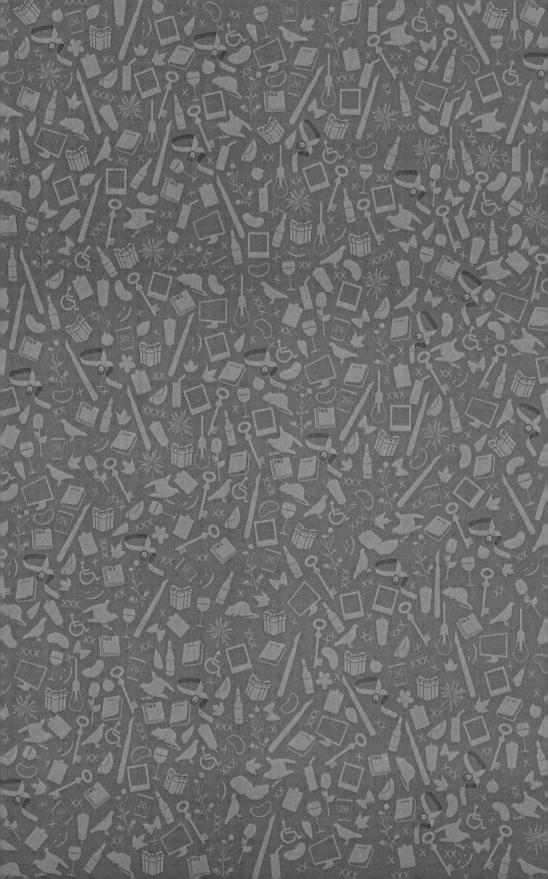

Lost in the Supermarket

"Code 8 to checkouts. Code 8 to checkouts please."

They said code 8 because they didn't want customers to know how they treated their skeleton staff. They were kids mostly. Kids and middle aged women. Apart from the greeter at the door – "Hello! My name's Alan and I'm here to help!" – most of the men worked in the upper echelons. Willie was the warehouse manager. He'd been a boxer once. You know, years ago, when it was a real sport. George ran the clothing department. Only beautiful females need apply. Any creed, religion, or race. Must be aged sixteen to twenty-one though. After that they stop trying. After twenty-one they don't care.

There were others too: Bakery Dave with his whooping cough, store manager Mike with football gear in the back of his company Jag and of course, Barry Miles. He was such a downwiththekids cunt that he made them all call him Milesey or Bazza. Some of the women from the staff canteen called him Bazooka. Stuff like, 'Full English for breakfast today, Bazooka?' Chances are he told them to call him that. Chances are it made him think about his cock.

For Cammy's first year and a half he managed to avoid checkout training altogether. The meat department was in the top corner of the store. As far away from the checkouts as you could get without hitting the warehouse.

Maybe because they were the only department that spent as much time off the shop floor as on it – cutting silverside into saleable chunks; slicing brisket; mincing the leftover ends – people tended to let them keep themselves to themselves. Maybe it was Barry. Maybe it was all of them. They had to deal with the fish counter as well and at store closing had to load the leftover fish stock into metal trays, three foot squared, then put them into an industrial chill. The next morning when they packed the counter with ice and presented the fish again, there was a residue on the steel trays that stank. Sometimes the guts would leak out. Organs had to be pulled out and binned.

Workers from their department could walk down the home hardware aisle and take any amount of scrubbing brushes, cloths or scourers they wanted. They had these special ones that Cammy sometimes hid. It was a scrubbing brush witha section where he could pour soap into so that it continually came out as he went at the trays. He had to turn the water up to boiling if he didn't want to be there until break time. All staff were meant to pay if they took anything from the shop floor. A woman from Beers, Wines and Spirits got shackled by security for taking a miniature of sherry down to the canteen to have with her birthday breakfast. She was sent home in tears the day she turned fifty. But it was different rules for the meat and fish staff.

The store had its own radio station which played songs on a three hour loop, announcing weekly deals and offers in between tracks. Soft rock was the theme of the day and as soon as the announcements about two-for-one-deals and how they were the cheapest supermarket for the whatever year running were over, the volume of the music didn't quite compare. They made the adverts louder than the tunes. Forced the customers to listen. The rest of the store might have been different but in Cammy's corner, with the buzz from the chills and the screeching of pallets going in and out the warehouse, it was hard to hear a thing.

"Code 8 to checkouts. That's a code 8 to checkouts please."

Julie from the deli, beautiful Julie with skin so golden, beautiful Julie who made the decision, after nine months of loyal service to the company, to start talking to Cammy – "You think you're such a rebel, don't you?" – beautiful Julie who he'd met up with before the Christmas night out for drinks. She'd had a few already. She took Cammy by the hand. He gave her money and watched as she strutted to the bar. Noticed how straight she held herself. Her slim shoulders. Then he watched other guys, actual adult men, watch her.

"You coming down to checkouts? You know he'll have you," Julie said.

"Who, Barry? Barry will have me? Good old Bazza?"

"You're acting tough now but we both know…"

She trailed off as she passed Cammy en route.

"Honestly Julie, tell him. Say I'm sitting on the shop floor with a reduction gun and putting all perishable items, including the silverside joints, down to 99p. Tell him."

She looked back over her shoulder.

"I will then," she said.

"I will then."

"Don't be so sarcastic, Cammy."

He stood on the spot as she wiggled off down the Beers, Wines and Spirits aisle. She did the side shuffle between two trolleys, her polo shirt getting caught and lifted just enough that it rode up and showed a part of her skin just above the apron. An old man turned to her and asked her a question. What time do you stop selling alcohol? That was a common one. What time do you start selling alcohol? Just as popular. On Sundays you could watch them waiting at the end of the aisle, minutes before twelve-thirty, fidgeting in the same way people would in the cold as they waited for the store to open.

Julie was nodding at the guy as he gestured with his hands. When she pointed him in Cammy's direction she did so with a smile. Cammy shook his head at her and mouthed 'How could you?'

"Code 8 to checkouts. Last call. Code 8 to checkouts please."

Julie looked up and drew her finger across her throat. Cammy shrugged. Then he pointed towards the checkouts and mouthed, 'Tell him. Tell him I'm…' He made a trigger finger and pointed to the chills. Julie narrowed her eyes and held her hand to her ear. Cammy mouthed it again slower, held the reduction gun up higher. She cupped her ear again then held her hands out in confusion.

"I'm saying tell him, Julie. Tell him I've got a gun."

Customers turned to stare. Julie pointed to her temple and looped a finger. Cammy's cheeks flushed and he moved closer to the chill. One of the lamb liver packets had burst open and there was brown blood dripping from one of the shelves. From above him came the sounds of the radio station – "Hello, Alan here! And today Ladies and Gents we have a special offer on Cottage Pie. Two for one on Classic Cottage Pie ladies and gents. And you can't say fairer than that."

"Fairer than that," Cammy said to himself. "Fairer than fucking that."

The old man Julie sent up was by his shoulder. He was stooped and frail.

"I heard you're the gent to speak to about the meat," he said.

Cammy stood up straight.

"Is that right?" the old man said.

"Yeah, sure. How can I help you?"

"Do you sell topside of beef?" he said.

Out the corner of his eye Cammy looked along the shelves. It was like they only sold topside of beef.

"We've a very wide selection. Is there any size in particular you're wanting?"

Cammy began to make my way along the chill. He held his palm down and outwards towards the meat.

"Because it all depends on how much you need. You want about 250g per person."

The old man said something so quiet it was hard to make it out.

"That's about half a pound in old money. Does that help?" Cammy said.

The old man had watery eyes and the red flesh beneath the eyeball went deep into his cheek. His eyelids drooped so far it was like he was displaying the inside of his face. There were yellow blemishes on the whites.

"It's for one son, you know," he said.

Cammy trawled through the pieces and lifted the smallest bit.

"How does this look?" he said.

The old man turned it over a few times in his hands. Lifted it to his nose and sniffed.

"I only normally cook for one," he said.

Cammy explained to the old man how to cook the meat. Told him that with topside what you wanted to do was seal it for a little while in butter. That some people, what they do is use oil, but if you use butter it gives it that extra bit of flavour. If the old man didn't have any flour in the house he should buy some. If he was to throw a wee bit of flour on the fat before putting the joint in the oven the fat would crisp up nicely. Cammy told him that was the way they did it in France.

"Flour, aye," he said. "Butter, I've got that."

"You'll be fine then," Cammy said.

There was a queue at the fish counter. Cammy went through to the back to get blue roll. He dipped into the meat chill through the plastic curtains. One day he had written his initials on one of the curtains. He'd written it in blood by dipping blue roll into the juice which ran from the cuttings. Barry made him clear it up after his shift. Called it a sign of disrespect.

Cammy used a good half of the roll on the spilt liver. It had leaked from the top shelf on to all four below it. It had spilt over beef olives, over the ready meals in foil trays then finished at the bottom and built a puddle on the lowest panels.

The old boy was still at the topside section picking through different pieces. Holding them up to his eye, peering at the label, holding them up to his nose for a sniff. In his trolley he had lots of tins. All he had was tins.

"You okay?" Cammy said.

He looked up.

"It's just the size son. I won't eat all that."

"I'll do you a little discount," Cammy said.

He went up to the fish counter. There was a queue of three or four – regulars, and he told them he'd be with them in a minute.

"They got you on yourself again?"

"How did you guess?"

The code for Haddock Fillet was 2366. You had to type it into the machine and a price came up. Cammy put in two pieces to get the right price. They had a roll of silver foil that could be folded to the size required and a machine welded it shut. Sometimes with a customer Cammy would raise the tray a little with his hand and trick it into thinking the weight was less than the actual. Or if someone said they wanted a Salmon fillet that cost a certain price he'd lift it just enough, hold his hand steady, and press print when the price was what they wanted.

"I've managed to do you a wee deal," he told the old man.

"What's that son?"

"Look."

Cammy handed him the silver packet and pointed at the price.

"What's it say?" the old man said.

"It's a staff discount. Quarter of the price. Even if you're not able to eat the whole piece you could cook it and then keep what you don't eat in the fridge. My Dad does that. Makes sandwiches for a few days afterwards. Roast beef sandwiches for his lunch."

"I don't understand," the man said.

"Look, just take it. It's okay."

The old man gave a nod. He walked off, pausing between steps. He walked like a wedding procession. Foot forward. Feet together. Other foot forward. Feet together.

Cammy finished serving at the fish then walked a few of the aisles. If James was about they'd be able to talk about some of the regulars. Buzz – the guy with the Bluetooth earpiece who'd only ever wear a NASA polo shirt; the odd couple – him old, fat and bald, her young, beautiful and Asian. James used to do impressions of them – "And what's this then dear?"

"Ahhhhpow. Ahhhhpow."

"Well done dear. Apple, yes. Good girl, good girl."

There were hardly any staff on the shop floor. Cammy snuck his phone out his pocket and checked the time. Six hours to go. He was in the Seasonal aisle and they had disposable barbeques stacked ten high in a hundred rows.

By the time he got to the last aisle at the top end of the store he still hadn't seen anyone he knew. Normally you heard Bakery Dave before you saw him but for once he wasn't spluttering all over the loaves.

"Alright," he said, "you not down at checkouts?"

"Nah man, they sent me back up."

"Aye?"

"Said they didn't need me."

He leant over to the cases of bread and started stacking them.

"You can help me then," he said.

"I can't man, sorry. I'm on the fish. If there's a queue, you know."

He spat air and shook his head.

"Skiving again Cammy, skiving again."

"You know me too well it seems sir."

He glared at Cammy.

"What you smiling at?" he said.

"Nothing man, I'm just saying."

Bakery Dave began to cough.

"Away and... Go and bloody..."

He was turning red, spitting phlegm onto loaves of bread.

"The fish... You're a..."

"Aye alright, I'm going man."

Cammy walked along the top deck past the pizza counter and the deli. Julie still wasn't back. Helen from Pizzas was flitting between customers and merchandise.

"And for you sir... And yourself madam... Yes sir... No problem madam..."

Cammy winked at her.

"You should be in here helping," she called.

"I can't Helen. Cooked meat and raw meat. Contamination. And the fish, you know."

Barry was on the counter when Cammy got back. He had his ponytail up in a hairnet and had put on his baseball cap and whites to serve. Cammy washed his hands and got to work.

Barry knocked into him as he was serving. His ponytail swished against Cammy's face. There were two scales, one either side of the fish counter, and normally there's enough space for two, but Barry was barging Cammy. As they made their way to the foil machine he was knocking Cammy off balance. Cammy dropped a salmon fillet on the floor.

"Barry mate, gonny watch," he said.

Barry pressed the lid down on the silver packet.

"Excuse me?" he said.

"You made me drop my salmon, man."

"Maybe you should be more careful," Barry said.

Cammy turned to the customer and apologised. He picked another from the ice and went to wrap it. Barry was still at the machine.

"When we're done here get downstairs."

"Cool mate, no bother."

"We need to have a serious chat."

Barry walked away and served the next in line.

Cammy gripped the bar of the machine. Licked the insides of his gums. Who the fuck did he think he was talking to? 'Cause he hadn't gone down to serve at the checkouts? Who'd be serving at the fish if he had?

Barry was at his back.

"You've some nerve," he said.

"What?"

"We'll talk about it downstairs," he said.

He stood so that Cammy had to squeeze past him. Cammy's voice was shaking when he served the next customer. She was a regular who always asked if she could have the little scrappy bits of whiting to give to her cats. They were the bits that nobody else wanted and normally they went to waste.

"Hello today," she said.

Cammy nodded.

"This weather eh?" she said. "Keep wondering if we'll get a summer."

"Is it still raining then?"

"It is, yes. It's kept up all day."

"I don't feel so bad about being stuck in here then," he said.

She smiled.

"So is it the usual for you?"

"Yep, just for the wee ones. Whatever you've got."

"How are they?" Cammy said.

"Oh they're fine. They were moaning and moaning this morning. That's them saying to me 'we want our fish'."

Barry was milling about behind Cammy.

"I'll just get you downstairs mate," Cammy said.

"I'll wait."

Cammy took the little bits and pieces and weighed them. He pointed the screen towards her.

"That okay?"

"Is that the price?" she said.

"That's the price," Cammy said.

Barry walked over. He directed his conversation to the old woman.

"Are we okay here?"

"Normally when I buy this it's very cheap but today... Have the prices gone up?"

"Is it these pieces you're wanting?" Barry said.

"They're for my cats."

He turned to Cammy.

"Did you put this through at full price?"

"Aye, course I did."

Barry turned to the woman.

"It was a mistake," he said.

Barry put his fingers under the scales and lifted then pressed the print button.

"Is that more like it?" he asked her.

The lady smiled. Barry knocked past Cammy and bagged up the fish. Cammy stood and shovelled the ice trying to fill in any gaps that had melted.

"Here you go now," Barry said. "Sorry about that."

The group conference room was where he'd been taken on the day of his interview. They'd had to do a group task, building a paper tower out of eight bits of paper that had to be a metre tall and freestanding. When Barry led him in it was the first time he'd been back.

"Sit down," he said.

Barry was holding a piece of headed notepaper and was writing something down on a separate pad.

"So?" he said. "Explain yourself."

"Look Barry, you've already made up your mind here so can we just get it over with."

"You're required to explain your actions. Are you aware of the severity of this situation?"

"Severity of the situation? Jesus Christ Barry. There were a thousand of you on checkouts. If I'd come down then there'd have been nobody to watch the fish. I was doing you a favour."

"I'm not talking about that."

He put his palms flat on the table and leant towards Cammy. "Why don't you tell me what's been going on? I'd like to know exactly what it is you've been up to today."

"Up to? I've been working here three and a half years."

"Exactly."

"Is it the gun thing?"

"For God sake, what the hell do you get up to on our time?" Barry said.

"What?"

"Look stop talking. I'm really sick of this Cameron. I shouldn't have to always be explaining your behaviour to other people. I've stuck my neck out for you again today. But it doesn't mean you can just think, ah Bazza. It's just Bazza. He won't mind. And then do what you want."

"This really feels like I'm doing what I want Barry."

"See that's your problem. If you shut it now then maybe this won't go any further."

Cammy stood up. Barry's eyes were on him.

"Congratulations then," Barry said. "Enjoy your written warning."

Cammy held his hand out.

"All I've done is try and help people," he said.

"Let's hope this isn't the beginning of the end, eh Cammy?"

Cammy took the piece of paper from him but Barry held the other end tight.

"Cheer up Cammy," he said.

"You got a pen?"

As Cammy signed, he felt Barry's hand on his back.

"It's nothing personal Cammy. It's policy."

"It always is."

On Cammy's way up to finish his shift he walked past the checkouts. Julie was on a far end system scanning items for a woman with three kids in tow.

"Look what I got," Cammy said.

She shook her head.

"Good old Bazza isn't so good after all," Cammy said.

"You had it coming."

Julie turned to the woman with the kids. One of them was darting past all the checkouts with his arms held out and making a noise like an aeroplane.

"Do you want a hand packing?" Cammy asked her.

"Aw that'd be great... Christopher!"

She ran up towards her son and Cammy helped the other two kids pack up the shopping.

"All I did was what I always do," he said.

"Just keep your head down for a while and don't do anything stupid," she said.

"You know, I just want to quit. You fancy it? We'll just walk out together. How much money you got saved?"

"I'm not walking out with you Cammy."

"We should. We should run away together. Do something that actually matters. Me and you. Go to the Gaza Strip or something. Help out the Palestinians. Or go to Africa. We need to fucking do something."

The wee boy looked up at him and pointed. "Oh ah, baddy," he said.

"Sorry wee man."

"You're so dumb," Julie said.

"Is it Uni that's stopping you? Just quit. If you quit I'll quit."

"I actually like working here though," she said.

"Yeah, we won't like it when we're forty."

"We won't be working here then."

"Well we'll be doing something just as bad. This is it, Julie."

"God Cammy, you're so much fun, so light hearted you know that. A total breath of fresh air."

"I'm just saying, if you wanted to quit then I'd quit."

"I don't want to quit."

Barry came up the stairs dressed in his whites. He tied his ponytail tight and began to walk towards the checkouts.

"Here we go," Cammy said.

"Just grin and bear it," Julie said.

Barry stood hands on hips and shook his head.

"Get on that fish."

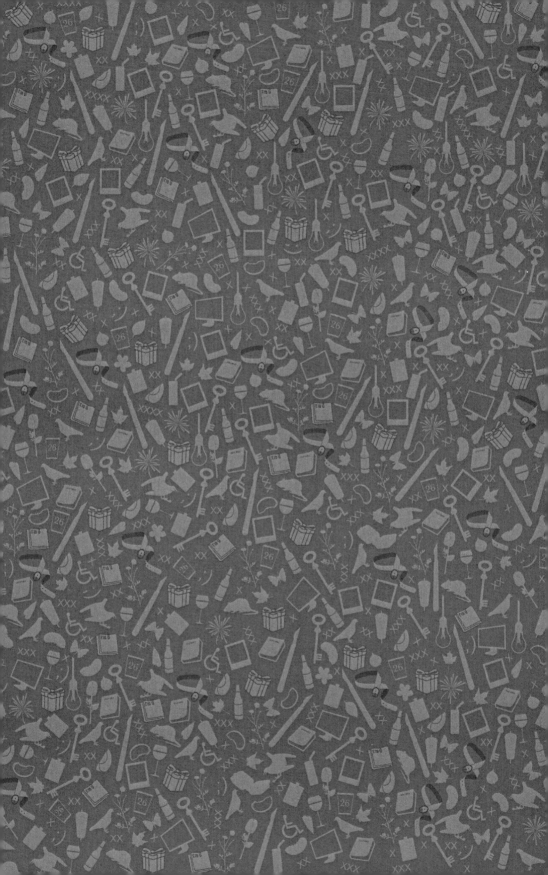

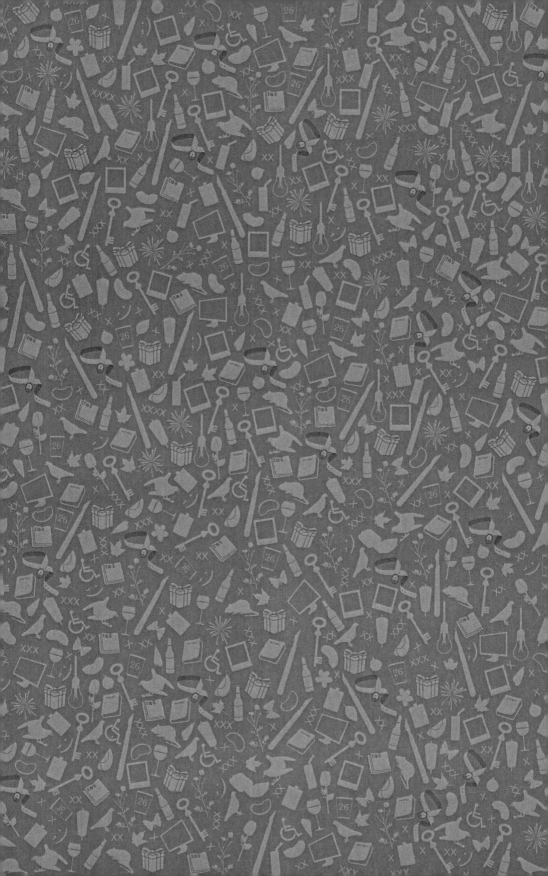

We are more than this

I'd had to walk two miles because the shop at the bottom of the road didn't have flowers. I ended up buying other things at the supermarket as well: a packet of bacon, pancake mixture, strawberries, maple syrup, lemon, sugar, Nutella, chocolates, a chick flick on DVD, a plant, one of those things that you crush herbs in, two light bulbs, wallpaper paste to fix the bit that was torn. And then there was the flowers.

"Look, is there no way we can come to some sort of arrangement? I'm in here all the time. You've seen me."

The girl smirked.

"I don't live that far. I'll go and get my wallet and bring the cash down."

"Oh aye, sure thing, no problem. We'll look after the shopping for you, that's fine."

"Aye, thanks, but it's just I'm needing some of the stuff now."

She licked her teeth before speaking.

"Here it comes. You chose the wrong checkout mate."

"Can I not just take it with me? There's things I need. I'll come back. I promise."

"Of course you will mate. Very good. Thanks but no thanks."

I leant across and placed my hand on her arm.

"Look doll, let me take the flowers. I'll come back down and pay for the rest but let me take the flowers now. That's all. Just the flowers."

"Doll?" she says, "Do I look like a doll?"

"Naw, I was just saying."

She shrugged my hand off.

"Cause that attitude will get you nowhere with me. Staff in this supermarket are here to work, not to be abused by members of the public."

"Let me take the flowers okay. How about I leave my jacket as insurance?"

She stood up. I don't know if she was on a raised platform or just bigger than me.

"Siobhan! Gonnae come down here."

A wiry, ginger-haired woman came marching down the aisle. She stood between me and the girl and looked up at each of us.

"Is there a problem here Lynne?"

"I'm no dealing with this Siobhan. I've told you before, I'm no dealing with these men. These... Men."

"Look, I was just saying to the girl, I've left my wallet and..."

"Are you abusing members of my staff?"

"It's just I've got to take these flowers. I'm needing to take the flowers but I've left my wallet in the..."

"Staff in this supermarket are here to work, not to be abused by members of the public."

"He's a jakey Siobhan. A jakey."

"I'm not a jakey! I work in pensions."

The girl took the woman's shoulder and turned her round to face.

"He called me doll Siobhan. I mean, dae I look like a doll tae you?"

"No you certainly do not." She turned back to face me. "This is the twenty first century pal. How dare you call a woman doll?"

The girl Lynne leant over the wee woman's shoulder.

"He's a chauvinist pig Siobhan."

"Aye you're a chauvinist pig," she said.

"Right look, look," I held my hands up in defence. "I didn't mean to hurt anybody's feelings. I just need the flowers and then I'll come back down." I took my jacket off. "Look, I'm going to leave this as insurance. I'll come back."

"We're not wanting your jacket," the supervisor says.

"I telt ye Siobhan; jakey"

"I'm really sorry."

I lifted the flowers from the trolley and walked away from the checkouts. They were shouting after me. They were shouting for me to stop, to stop right now or they'd call the police. I started to run. I ran past women pulling their children towards them. An old man tried to trip me with a trolley. I ran and I ran. When I had the courage to look back I was through the car park and on the street. There was nobody following. I bent over, laid the flowers on the pavement and tried to get my breath back.

The sweats started as I walked home. It might have been the run, but it felt like it was guilt dripping out of me. I thought about the previous night. About how Amy was when I got in. I woke in the night sensing she was awake. It was hard to take that. It was hard to think that I could make someone that angry.

There's an Arab Strap song that goes, "And every night a taxi softly sneaks you up our street, you used to say you'd broke your phone, now you don't care if you're discreet." And that other song that goes, "I think my missus is fucking every guy that she looks at." These repeat in your mind when you least expect. Seeing her face in your head. Her face, his face. Eyes touching like fingers.

Every so often I glanced over my shoulder but the street was empty. The walk home was quiet. I started getting cold and thought about ditching my jacket like that. It'd been a present from her Mother. One of those herring bone wool coats. It must have cost her. One hundred, two hundred pounds maybe. I didn't wear it that much anymore but it was a nice coat. Good for the winter. Good for special occasions. And with it being dark it was good for funerals. I'd worn it to my Grandmother's funeral. And I wore it to Amy's Grandmother's funeral too.

It was only when I turned into our street that I heard the sirens. There must have been about five police cars and a wagon. Two ambulances as well. It was further up the street where they gathered. There were two young policewomen pulling the police tape round cones and cordoning off a square area. Inside the cordoned off section there was one of those white tents you see on the news that they put over bodies at a murder scene.

When I saw the tent I knew. I looked around. There were people covering their mouths with their hands. Witnesses were talking to the police and making wild gestures to show what had gone on. She'd jumped. I could see that now. She'd gone out the living room window. Four floors. Her head had hit the ground and splattered.

Maybe that's when I dropped the flowers, I don't know. But I realised then. I wished there was somebody there I could share that realisation with, but everyone was a stranger. I could see my future. I'd get two weeks off work for grieving. Maybe they'd give me more on compassionate grounds. I'd just

have to get a note from the doctor, lay it on thick. Three months would be nice.
I could go travelling. I'd miss people's birthdays and forget what age I am. I'd drink
too much and take every drug I could find. And I'd take a camera. Document it all.
Sell it when I got back, if I ever came back. Title it something like *Life After Death:
One Man's Quest*, and sell it to Channel 4.

A plain clothed police officer pulled me aside and asked me what I'd seen.

"Nothing," I told her. "I didn't see anything. I just got here."

She told me how it seemed that the woman just hadn't seen the wee boy.
That he'd chased a football onto the road and that she never even touched
the brake until his body landed. She was distraught, this woman. Inconsolable,
she said. And yes, there'd be a full investigation. If it was considered negligence
on her behalf then she'd be punished. The boy was six years old.

When I got into the flat Amy was still in bed. She was rubbing sleep from
her eyes.

"What's going on outside?"

"A wee boy got knocked down."

She sat up.

"A woman hit him with her car. I think he's dead."

"Please say you're joking Ian. Please tell me you're making this up."

"I'm not."

She made to get up.

"Don't," I said. "Stay in bed. It's horrible. Don't look, please."

She began to cry.

"I can't believe this, I really can't believe this."

"Just let's lie here. Put on a DVD or something."

She covered her face with the pillow. I sat down and put my hand on her back.

"What the fuck is happening?" she said.

"I'm sorry," I said, "It's all my fault."

When I stood up she twisted to look at me.

"Don't go Ian. Don't fucking leave now."

"I've got to," I said.

"If you go now that's it. I mean it. That's it for good."

"I bought you flowers," I said.

"We're more than this, Ian, okay? Go later. Don't go now."

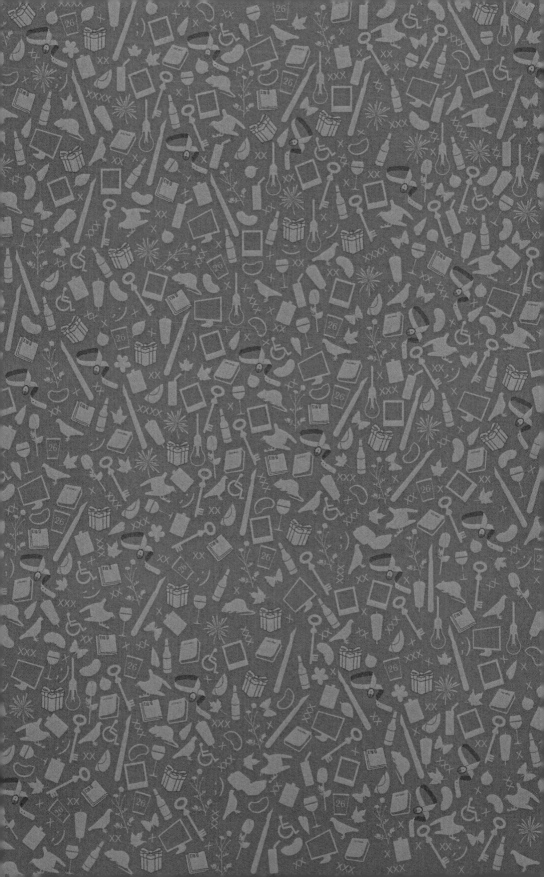

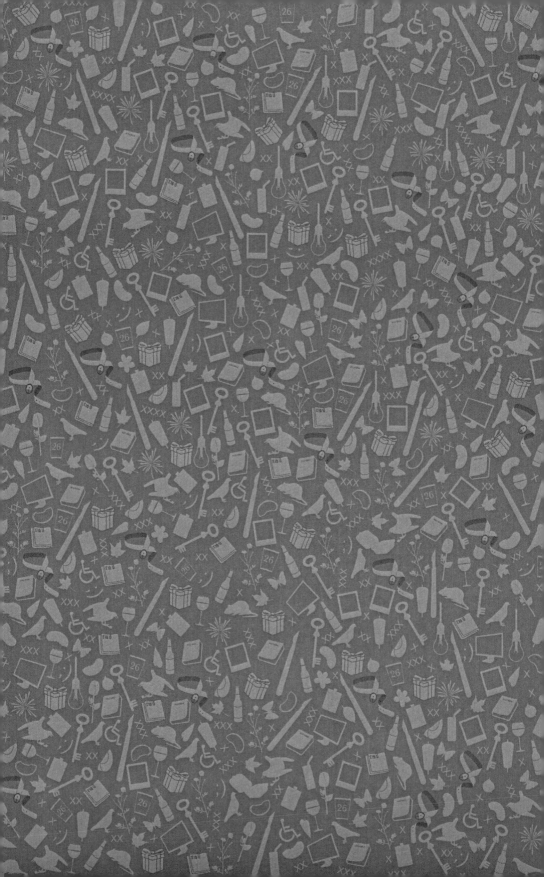

Black 26

The couple ran from one doorway to the next. The rain fell heavily. Even in the five or so steps between doors the water soaked through to their skin.

"Please trust me. I feel lucky tonight," the girl said.

"We can't miss this bus. Miss this and we're walking home." He pointed from the doorway to the black sky. "In this."

She stood on one foot ready to make a run for the next door along. He put an arm on her shoulder and pulled her back. Strands of her hair stuck to his face.

"You've got ten minutes," he said. "If you're not back here in ten minutes, I'm telling you, we'll miss it. No joke. You know what it's like at this time."

"I know," she said, "but I've never had this feeling before."

She took his hand in hers and leant forward. She ran ahead of him and as her heels threw up splashes they wet the front of his jeans. Her dress was sticking to her thighs. When they reached the bus stop he pulled her under the shelter and pressed her against the Perspex.

"There's steam coming off your head," she told him.

She wiped his forehead with the back of her fingers, moving the fringe out of his eyes.

"You better get going," he said.

The road was so wet that the whole piece of tarmac, from their side to the other, looked like it was part of the drainage system. Lights from clubs, takeaways, twenty-four hour newsagents, reflected their colours on the water. When a taxi drove over, or a person ran through, the puddles changed and the colours looked wrong.

She kissed him. "And you're cool with it if I go?"

"Just as long as you're back in time to catch the bus."

"I'll be five minutes. I know what I'm doing. Number 26."

"Number 26 is black."

"Okay, thanks. Black."

"Why number 26?" he said.

"It was a good year. When we were twenty-six."

"You think?"

"I thought so."

He shrugged. "Glad I'm not old."

"Keep telling yourself that."

"Come on," he said, pulling her closer. "I could still pass for twenty-six, right?"

She kissed him on the lips and took his hands from her waist.

"So I get the chips from the dealer and then I put it on my number? Then the dealer spins it and when the ball lands on my number I win?"

"Just make sure that you put your money down in enough time otherwise you'll have to wait until the next round of betting. If you don't bet quickly enough then you lose your chance."

"I'm betting it all. How do I know if I'm too late?"

"Because the dealer will say something. He'll say something like no more bets or money down and then you know."

"Okay, okay," she said, "I get it."

She stepped back and turned the other way. In the back of her dress, where he'd had his arms, there were patches that were stuck tighter to her skin. The way the rain had made her hair brought it down one side of her neck and over the shoulder. At the other side you could see the skin, its tiny hairs standing on end. She had a pink bra strap visible and the black strap of her dress had slipped to the side, hanging out in a hoop.

"Do you want my jacket? At least if you've got my jacket then you'll be warm."

"It's a bit late for that," she said, "I doubt I'll ever be warm again."

He reached for her shoulder.

"I should have given you my jacket earlier. I'm sorry. I should have given you it. That's what I should have done. If I'd given you my jacket like I'm supposed to do then maybe this wouldn't be happening."

"Giving me your jacket wouldn't make a difference. I wasn't cold anyway. It's just now, right when we started standing here, that I felt cold. Up until now I hadn't felt cold. But I do now."

"You should take it then. Even if you just wrap it around you. If you're not wanting to actually put it on. The jacket is soaking anyway. I can feel the rain getting in."

"I should probably go now."

He got his phone from his pocket and checked the time.

"You've got ten minutes still. Probably in this weather the bus will be late anyway or at the worst come on time. If you go now we've still got time."

"Okay," she said. She took a deep breath and moved a step forward. She stopped and turned to him. "Are you sure you're okay about the money?" she said. "I mean I don't want to spend it if you're not okay with it. It's nothing to do with you at all. You know that. It's just 'cause I've got this feeling. Number twenty-six."

"My age," he said.

"You've used that joke already."

He shrugged. For a while they stood like that and then he shook his head and spoke.

"I'm fine with it. Honestly I am. I just don't want to see you getting hurt."

She raised her hands in the air.

"Why do you have to be so negative all the time? I've never had this feeling before. Never. I'm not a silly wee girl. I know that if I get this feeling then I've got to go with it. I'm not saying that I'll definitely win, I'm saying I feel like I'm going to. Can you not see that? Don't you get it?"

"No," he said. "I really don't."

He squinted to see through the condensation in the Perspex. In the distance lots of headlights from cars, taxis and buses lit the street in glare. If anything, the water seemed to be making everything brighter.

"I'm just going to run across now."

He was staring in the direction the bus would come from when she walked away.

"I'll be really quick. You don't have to be like that. I'll be really fast. If I win I'll buy us something special."

He didn't acknowledge that she'd spoken. Maybe he hadn't heard.

"Black twenty-six," she called back. "Just wait and see. It's you and me and black twenty-six."

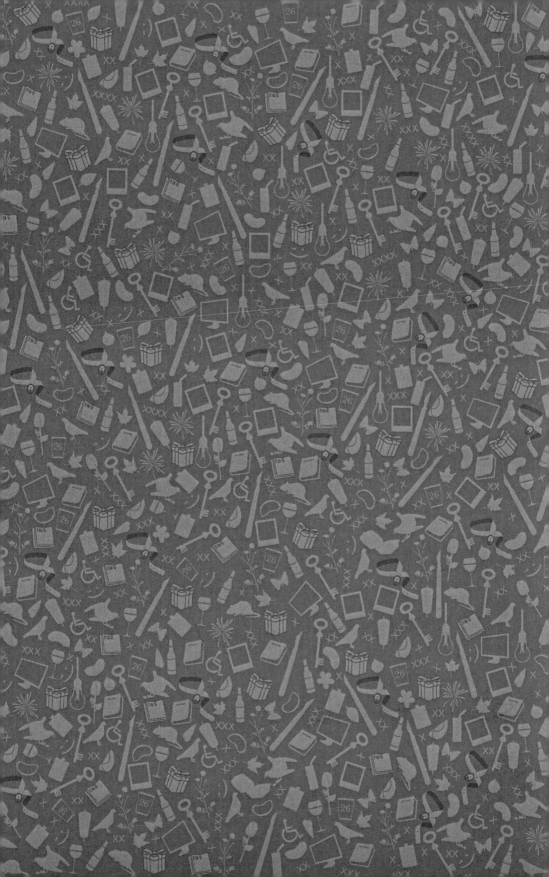

Important Things to do

The pigeons would only eat what the seagulls did not. There were many seagulls and maybe five pigeons to each seagull. But they did not hassle the seagulls. They waited for their turn to eat. When it was their turn they ate quickly. They fought amongst themselves for the food that was left.

Steven was not really wanting to see this type of thing. He was drunk.

It was that time on a Spring morning when it is light enough to seem beautiful. He did not know the time because he did not wear a watch. He had thrown his mobile phone into a line of oncoming traffic sometime in the twelve hours previous.

No other people. No cars or taxis. A fifteen minute window. Maybe less. Polystyrene cartons had not been removed yet. Empty bottles, half eaten burgers, chips, rolls. Circles of sick in alleyways and in-shots. Soon the people who were paid to deal with these things would come. For now it was something to enjoy. To watch the birds eat. To close his eyes, hear their squawk and believe he could be at sea, on a boat. Going somewhere. Anywhere. Emigration.

He looked at the bus stop's digital screen. It was broken. He shrugged. He was no longer to be constrained by such trivialities as time. He knew it was possible. Possible for the North Koreans and the Israelis. They did not choose to use the Gregorian calendar like everybody else. In North Korea it was not the 21st Century. What was it in North Korea? Year seventy fucking six or something? Who knew, but the balls to do that.

It must have been nearly six o'clock. In three hours he would have to be... Aye. So: home, shower, shave then that'd be it over. The end of the revolution. Fin de Siecle, fin du monde. He would reach the office, a thin carpeted building where swipe cards gained you entry in and out of most nearly every room, including the entrance, kitchen and pisser. That someone could go to the bathroom six, seven times per day. Heavens.

There was time to make it. The sit down at the bus stop had provided clarity. The intimate detail in which he watched the birds allowed his knowledge of being alone to become a lucid realisation of sobriety and yes he had drank. But there was time. Nobody would ever know. There were days when he could swipe in, work at the computer screen, do one task, mark it complete, do another task, mark it complete. Do another task. Eat lunch. Eat at the computer screen. Check out Facebook, Twitter, BBC news, livesportontv.com. Stare at Easyjet, Ryanair. In the afternoon work again. At five thirty go home. You don't have to speak to another person some days. They can't smell you over email.

What was the problem? Maybe that light. Was that the biggest issue? Pointing down at his skull. The bulb was fucked. Was it creating some chemical imbalance in his psyche? Like not getting enough sunlight in winter. A lack of vitamin D. Some such nonsense, these thoughts. There was nothing metaphysical about his condition. Life didn't let you get metaphysical. He almost had the nerve to tell people about his belief that there were varying degrees of heat coming from it. Radiation perhaps. The light. When it flickered he could feel the temperature change. Light then dark. Going from one to the other a thousand times a day. Waking. Asleep.

Facing a computer screen. Beyond that a row of other peoples' backs and their screens. There was a window, but that was behind. If you looked behind, people just thought you'd been fantasising about them. All the gossip that started. Smilers asking you who you're shagging anytime you wanted to photocopy a fax from Arizona. Who you shagging? Did you hear who she shagged? You're not going to believe who she shagged.

On the Monday he had sent emails to Human Resources. You have to email maintenance directly, they said. Maintenance said they had to receive direct instructions from Human Resources. He forwarded them the email from Human Resources. Did Steven not understand? They needed direct correspondence from Human Resources. Not email forwards. On the Wednesday, that morning, he had taken to asking other people in the office. They shrugged or said they hadn't noticed the light.

He went so far as to email head office in the hope that perhaps, even remotely, people in a different country would be sensitive to his plight. Would care enough about a senior administrative clerk in Glasgow Branch number two. One of four branches in Scotland. 31 branches in the UK. Thousands in the universe. Perhaps someone in Arizona cared enough about him. He even emailed the boss man! And received an out of office reply from a woman called Jolene! Oh to have someone ignore your emails via proxy.

There didn't have to be a catalyst. Was that true? There had just been a parliamentary election. A vote in which not even half of the possible voting public voted for the ruling coalition of their pre-determined nation. Was he Scottish? Great British? Whatever. What a fucking arbitrary thing to be proud of. The next five years. Steven did not vote. Things really do not matter. He didn't speak about it. If people asked he'd tell them. Some said: "People gave their lives so you could get the vote!" People with a sense of right and wrong. The belief that they were doing something. About as radical as a sausage. So was he for that matter. Where were John Baird, James Wilson, Andrew Hardie, now? We have Steven, a lorne sausage of a man.

In the Perspex that shielded the bus timetables was the silhouette of his head and shoulders. He ran a hand through his hair and it flopped back down. He had reached an age where he was certain he should start going to a real hairdressers. A barber was okay for boys but for a man of fleeting youth and in his position it was really worth getting a proper haircut. What a stupid thing to think. An age when you should attend a real hair salon. Maybe he was balding a little. Male pattern baldness is unavoidable after all.

He checked his wallet. He brought out the folded notes. Counted twice. Eighteen twenties first time. Seventeen twenties the next. Losing count. Good problem to have. A lucky night. The croupier said so. Put the money away. That'd buy a new suit. He had a black one and a grey one but navy would be nice. With summer coming. A sky blue shirt. Or maybe a new TV. A guy in the work had a 50inch. It was shite having just a 32inch. You couldn't tell people. They'd say you canny watch anything on a 32inch. You need at least a 42inch. And you might as well get HD. Or even 3D. You seen that Avatar on 3D? You've got to see that Avatar on 3D.

He closed his eyes.

Anywhere, he thought. That was true. To use only the senses of taste, touch and sound. Synaesthesia, was that the word? This could be anywhere in the world. A cold night in Dundee, a stag weekend in Blackpool, a sunset in Tenerife.

He could not truly picture the last one. He opened his eyes. The Seagulls had gone. The pigeons ignored him. They were fighting amongst themselves.

He heard the bum before he smelt him. And when he saw him, it was only the feet and bottom half of his legs at first. The parts of the man that could be seen through the Perspex and beneath the timetable.

And he really was a bum. Not a junkie. Not a jakey. An out and out bum. It was the suitable word. Steven could see his trainers, flapping open at the front like a mouth. His faded jeans, baggy at the bottom, blown out by the breeze and too short for him so you saw his tattered skin. He was singing, "Ah belong tae Glasgow, dear auld Glesga toon. There's something the matter wae Glesga for it's gaun roond an roond..." Steven sat facing forward, pretending to be engrossed in any other detail. Maybe the bus would come soon and he could get on before the bum started talking to him. But what bus? To where? Maybe it'd be better sitting here all day. The people he'd meet. Maybe there'd be a woman of wealth who'd invite him home.

"You got a smoke pal?"

Steven pretended not to have heard.

"A smoke pal? Comprende? No speaka da English?"

Steven turned to the bum. He shook his head.

"So it's like that is it? I've got my own fags anyways pal. Don't you worry about me."

Steven listened as the bum went through his pockets. When he stopped, Steven turned around. The bum didn't have a smoke. Steven looked away, rubbed his face in his hands to wake himself up.

"You not speaking?"

"Tired mate," Steven said. He sniffed. Stayed still.

The bum walked past him. Past his back and into the bus stop entrance. He wheeled his trolley in first. Kicked the wheel so it was horizontal, jamming the trolley from rolling away. Then he sat down.

"I thought you were a smoker."

Steven shook his head.

The bum began to take his shoes off. He threw them it into his trolley. The trolley was already full. There were boxes. They looked empty. And a coat. There was another pair of shoes, packed neatly in the trolley's front section. They were in worse condition than the ones he'd been wearing. Black boots with no laces or sole. But shiny on top. Shiny so if you were standing still in them, a pair of trousers tucked over the tongue, they'd look quite smart. It was only when you walked, lifted one foot in front of the other, that people would see your toes.

He'd be carrying a knife. Someone like him. A man of the streets. Living that way. He'd be carrying a knife and know how to use it.

The bum started fiddling with his gloves. Pulling them off with his teeth. Pair after pair. His hands so fat under each, getting skinnier as they unravelled. When they were off you saw his hands weren't fat at all. They were veiny and skinny like pigeon feet. Frail little fingers that glowed red now they were out of the gloves. He began to rub his feet. Steven watched all this out the corner of his eye. If he wasn't a bum, would he be good looking? If he was young, still in his thirties or twenties, would he be better looking than Steven? If he wasn't a bum, would he be a good looking man? It was impossible to say for sure. You could not tell anymore. He was a bum.

There was a smell to the bum but it was just an outdoor smell like when Steven had come in after a run. He didn't smell like cheese or any of those things you normally associate with such bums. He rubbed his feet and said, "Oh, that's better."

"So what's your story? Coming or going?" the bum said.

"Going," Steven said.

"You get lucky wi some wee lassie?"

"Nah, not last night."

The bum began to laugh. It was a cackle. Like a guy with no teeth laughing.

"I'm just joking you pal. Just havin a wee laugh. You got a name?"

"Steven."

"Steven? Me too ma man!"

He held out his hand for Steven to shake it.

"Everybody calls me Stevie. They go like that," he cupped his hands around his mouth, "Stevie gees a song! Stevie, Stevie gees a song!"

He shouted it across the street. Shouted so loud that the pigeons flew away. Then he coughed.

"Or Steph. Some cunts call me Steph."

In the distance there was a low rumbling. It was hard to tell what it was. If it was a bus coming, or the bin lorry. It could have been a plane. Not close enough to involve itself in the affairs of the two men. Just a warning on the horizon that soon the new day would start.

That new government. One day they're saying there's no social mobility anymore. You'll die where you were born. Next day they're telling us to strive for more. Get involved and that. A better life for your family. One lifetime isn't long enough to become great. You need your parents to do better. Then you've got a chance. To start from nothing, the only hope you've got is for your children and their children after you're gone. Trying to make the next day more successful than the present or previous. Arizona man! Being physically in decline with each new day. Knowing that is hard. Trying to improve with that knowledge that you're expiring. Not admitting that. To people.

Was he thinking or speaking aloud? The bum was nodding his head. He opened up his jacket and brought out a brown, labelless bottle.

"Get some of that down you Stevo ma man."

Steven did. He took the bottle and downed the lot. It was a taste he hadn't experienced. It could have been draincleaner. But it was too late now.

The rumbling was getting louder. Maybe it was at the far end of the street. At Charing Cross. Clearing up the mess there. Then it'd move up and clear the section the two men sat at. Move up and clear the whole city.

"You werney meant to have it all Stevo fuck sake!"

Steven burped.

"Fucking hell Stevo ya bastard. You're a right bastard Stevo. That was to last me. Stevo. Fuck sake man."

Steven started to laugh. Then he brought out his wallet. Threw the bum two of the notes. Laughter like vomit. Tears blurring his vision. Rolling down his cheeks. The bum picked the notes up off the floor and pulled his shoes on.

"That's it Steph ya mad cunt. You get those bad boys on. And-a-lay, an-da-lay! Arriba, arriba!"

The bum was muttering under his breath. Gripping his shoes. Their flapping tongues and his toes sticking out the end. Steven pointed at him and the laughter went on.

"Ya mad weirdo Stevie. I gave you ma drink. Away you to fuck!"

The bum didn't even put on his gloves. He stuffed them into the coat pocket where he'd had the bottle stashed. He booted the wheel of his trolley until it was straight and he turned the whole contraption to face the pavement. He walked away quickly up the street, away from Steven and away from the noise heading their way. He ran from the rising sun, its gleam on his back, glinting off the trolley. Making the metal shine. He turned around every few steps, giving Steven the finger, shouting abuse, "Ya fuckin mad dafty!" and then he turned a corner and was gone.

A minute later the men came, using their brushes to sweep away the rubbish. They swept around Steven's feet. They swept up the polystyrene, the chips, the sick.

A minute after that the first bus came. Men in suits and carrying umbrellas on their arm. A young woman in a pencil skirt and blouse with buttons undone got off. She glanced at Steven then turned, walking fast, her heels echoing off the concrete.

And then Stephen knew he had to go home. He had to get home. Get ready quickly so as not to be late for work. He had things to do! Important things to do!

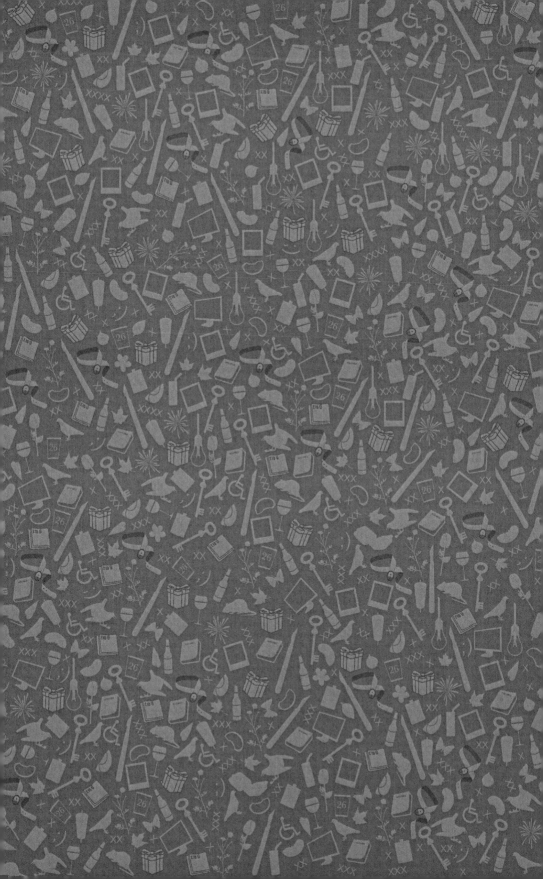

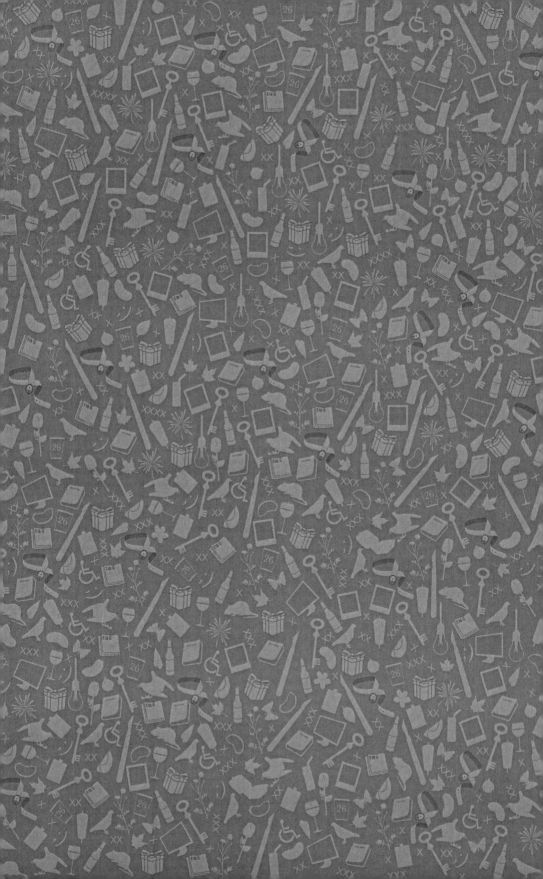

After the Party

Jane took my hand and placed it on her stomach. She said the baby was kicking hard.

"She keeps kicking, do you feel it? She's kicking to get out."

"Won't be long now," I said.

"It's like someone knocking, that's kind of what it feels like. Like fists knocking inside of me."

Jane took my hand again and moved it to a different part of her stomach. "Feel it here. Can you feel?"

I laughed and told her I could. We sat like that for a minute and she held on to my hand.

Tommy was sitting against the wall with his feet up on the bed. His eyes were shut.

"Tommy Tucker you dirty fucker. Are you asleep?" I said.

Tommy opened his eyes, squinted, then nodded his head.

"Aye, I am. So be quiet."

"Tommy, Tommy, Tommy Tommy Tucker, go get us some beers, you dirty, dirty fucker. Get up and bring us some more beers man, eh?"

Jane hit me on the arm. "Shoosh, not in front of the baby."

Tommy stretched his hands behind his neck and groaned. "None left mate.

I checked twenty minutes ago."

"Tommy, Tommy, Tommy. Do you really think your man here would be dumb enough not to have backups? Washing machine."

Tommy shook his head. "Mate, I'm sick of drinking. I want to go home."

I pushed his feet off the bed and he tutted.

"Och, go on Tommy," said Jane. "Do it for me. You wouldn't want to upset a pregnant woman would you? You wouldn't want me to walk down those stairs in my condition. Would you? What if I was to fall? What then Tommy?"

Over the top of her I'm singing. I'm leaning over my lap and pointing my face towards him. "Tommy Tommy Tucker, stop being a fucker, get the drink ya stupid prick and stop being a... fucker."

Jane came close to me. She covered my lips with her fingers.

"Is that really what you want Tommy?" she said. "Really? Even though I'm naming the baby after you. Even if it's a girl? You'd really grudge getting him those tiny little beers?"

Tommy was messing about with a marker pen. He had written 'love' on one fist and 'hate' on the other.

"Would you Tommy? Would you want me to go down there in my condition?" Jane said.

"Aye okay, okay. Christ, see you pregnant women. You're lucky you're pretty."

Tommy stood up and feigned to hit me.

"You just shut it bawbag or I'll be on you with this pen again."

I looked at my arm, licked my finger and wiped it. The ink didn't smudge.

"It's a permy ya dick," Tommy said. He lifted his arms and stretched. "Anybody got the time?"

Jane leant over and took her phone from the top of the TV.

"Oh God, it's nearly four in the morning."

"What time did you think it was?"

"I didn't think. That means it's only... twelve days to go. Can you believe that? Twelve days."

"Not long," I said.

"And you're still looking that slim and sexy as well," said Tommy. "Jane, you're an inspiration. My bird is fatter than you and she's not even pregnant."

He was standing turning his neck from side to side. Above the song from the laptop speakers you heard it crack.

"It'll fuckin be here before the beers if you don't stop wasting time," I said.

"Oooooh," goes Tommy, "time of the month is it bawbag? Are you listening to this guy Jane? Can you believe he's speaking like that in front of your wee baby?"

"You know what Tommy, I can't. I really expected more from this one. He'd never have spoken that way to me when we were younger, don't you agree?"

Tommy was smirking.

"It really is no way to behave in front of a lady."

"Thank you Thomas," said Jane.

I copied her voice.

"Fuck you Thomas," I said.

This time he went to slap me and caught my cheek. When it landed it sounded more like a crack than a slap.

"Fuck sake man, that was really sore."

"Aww, has little baby Sam got a little sore face?"

He was laughing. Jane was too.

I gave him the finger.

"Right, beers then," Tommy said. He walked towards Jane saying, "Bye baby, bye, bye."

He got in close, lifted her top and put his lips on her stomach. Then for a few seconds he rubbed where the baby was, let his hand rest there, and nobody spoke.

"Right," I said. "Beers Tommy?"

He stood up quickly and nodded to me.

"Remember? Washing machine. And see whilst you're down there, go and take the dog a walk or something."

Jane spoke before Tommy got the chance.

"He's right Tommy. Would you? Please? It'd be a massive favour. My Mum and Dad will go crazy if he's not been walked. Even if you just walk him around the garden until he's done his business."

Tommy left the room then stuck his head back around the door.

"Just make sure you name that baby after me then."

"Of course," Jane said.

When he was gone she said, "Can't believe I lost touch with you lot. Tommy's still such a good guy isn't he?"

"Aye. If you like lazy, arrogant twats."

"Jealous, Sam?"

"Of him?"

She didn't answer me. Instead she looked at her phone again and said, "It was so weird bumping into you guys last night. Do you think there will be anybody still in the house? I hope nothing's wrecked. My Mum and Dad will go crazy."

"Probably," I said. "Maybe like Jamie, Gibby and that. One or two of the girls."

I stood up from the bed and went over to the window. I pulled back the curtain and looked out to the garden. Tommy wasn't there. I asked Jane if she minded me smoking.

"As long as you do it out of the window."

I sparked up the cigarette and sucked it in.

"Here, remember the buzz you used to get from smoking? Like when we were wee? Remember how good it was?"

She shrugged.

"Yeah, I suppose. Remember how we used to say twos, threes, ld's and all that? Remember when we used to go round to your granny's just to 'borrow' her cigarettes and we'd hide round the back at the bins and smoke all of them?"

"Do you remember what else went on at those bins?" I said.

Jane looked away.

"What? Shy all of a sudden are we?"

She didn't answer.

"Because you weren't shy then."

"You wanting punched? 'Cause I'll do it."

"Just saying, the things you knew at sixteen."

"Stop it, Sam," she said.

I looked out to the garden. Couldn't stop myself from smiling. I finished my fag and dropped the butt out the window. It slid down the slates and finished up in the gutter. When I turned round she was leant back on the bed with her hands resting on her stomach. Her eyes were closed, the lashes fluttering as her hands moved over the baby.

"You're not really going to call your baby Tommy, are you?" I said.

She shook her head.

"Because you know, Sam is actually a boy's name or a girl's name. So you could call the baby Sam. I don't mind giving you my name."

"Yeah, very good. I'm sure that will go down well with Derek. He'll just love me calling our baby after..."

"The father?"

She opened her eyes.

"Ha ha, very funny. No. I could never name him after you. He's really jealous actually."

"Seriously? Of me?"

"No. Just of things in general. Of my life before him. He says that he's angry at himself for not meeting me sooner."

"That's slightly mental, Jane."

She sat forward and pointed at me. "It's not. It's romantic."

"Romantically mental. What's the deal with that? How can the guy deny you, deny you... A past?"

"Very deep Sam."

"Well you know what I mean. It's nobody's fault that you didn't meet him earlier. That's just life. Does he not understand that?

"He loves me."

We were quiet for a while.

"I loved you."

"We were kids, Sam."

"So?"

Jane pointed at the cock that had been drawn on my arm.

"You're still a kid," she said.

"That was Tommy. Honestly, I had nothing to do with it."

Jane shook her head. I lit up another cigarette, put my head out the window and sucked it in. Then I turned around to Jane. "I can't believe he's jealous man. That's funny. You've been with the guy what, five years?"

She lay back on the bed, twirled her hair around her fingers and said, "It's just he wanted to be my first."

I sucked in air through my teeth.

"Well sweetheart, he might have everything else, but I'll always have that."

She rolled her eyes. "That, unfortunately, is true."

"Oi!" I started walking over to the bed. "What's that meant to mean?"

I sat beside her and tickled her underarms. She pulled back.

"I'm going to shout rape if you don't stop touching me up!" she said.

"Rape? Very good." I leant in close and moved my hand onto her leg, squeezing just above the knee, just at the pressure point that always made her laugh.

"Stop it," she said, "it's tickly."

She was squirming about, moving towards the wall. I moved my fingers further up her leg, pressing on all the points. Touching through her leggings and under her dress. Moving up and pressing.

"Sam, fuck sake! Stop I said."

Her voice sounded grown-up.

"Look, just stop ok. You can't do that. I told you to stop and you wouldn't. Don't forget I'm pregnant."

She moved to sit upright against the wall. She was struggling to get up so I took her hand to help.

"I'm fine," she said, knocking my hand away. "I don't need your help."

I backed away from her and sat half off her bed. She straightened her clothes and put her hands on her stomach again. "Can you pass me my phone please."

When I gave her it she began tapping the keys. It looked like she was writing a text.

"Are you okay?" I said.

She dropped the phone by her side. It bounced a couple of times then settled on the duvet.

"Look, it's just..." she sighed. "I don't know, it's just weird. Last night fun, but this... I'm sorry."

I stood up and went over to the window. It was getting light outside. It was a few minutes before either of us spoke.

"Were you texting Tommy?" I said.

"What? No. Why would I be texting Tommy?"

"I dunno. 'Cause you want him back here?"

She sat up again.

"I don't even have Tommy's number. Why would you think I'm texting Tommy? Why are you even saying that?"

I turned away from her towards the window. Soon I'd have to go home. The flat was a mess. I'd a guy coming round to have a look at the pipes. There was a smell coming from the plughole. Whenever I turned the washing machine on the whole place stank of eggs. It'd been getting worse over time. I had to tidy the flat for the guy coming round. I had to go home.

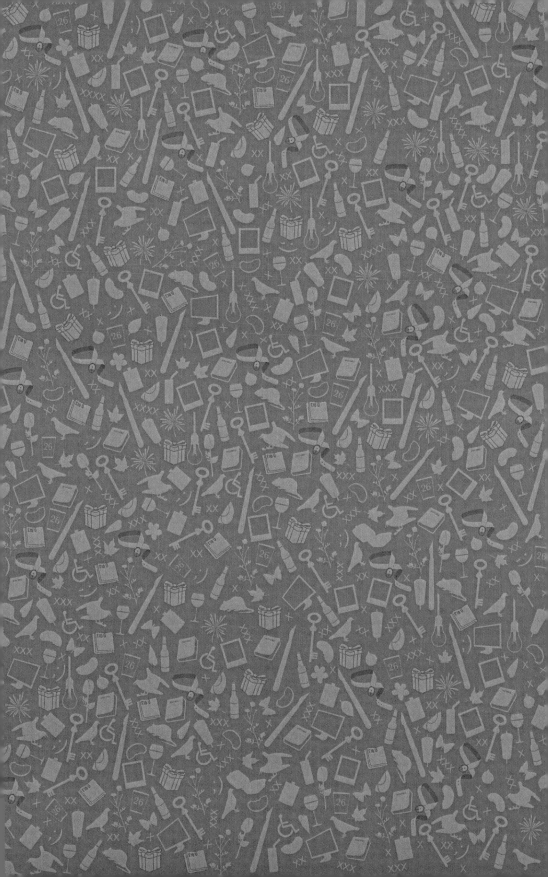

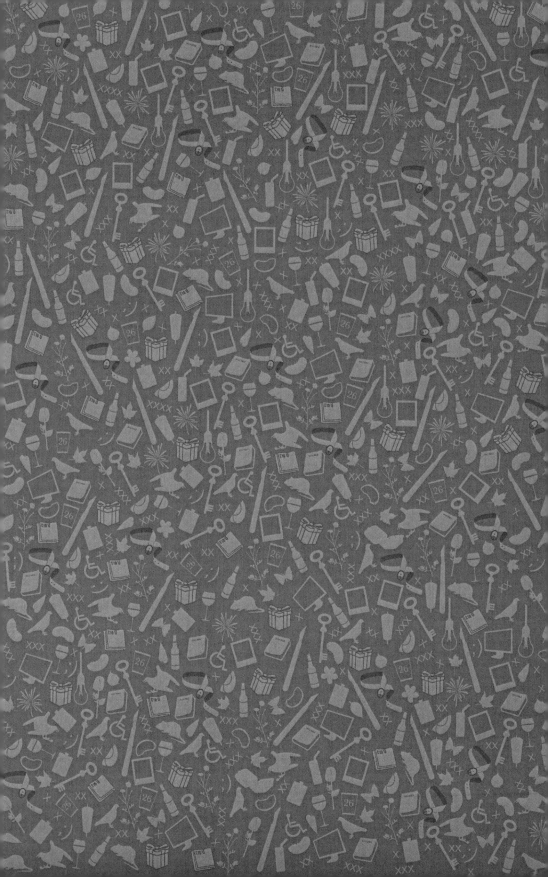

A Couple

I sat up when Annie turned the light on.

"You jumped up there," she said.

"I was already awake."

Annie sat by my feet and took the towel off her head. Her hair was wet and tangled.

"I dreamt I was missing a tooth," I said. "It was funny. I looked in the mirror and right in the front of my mouth there was a tooth missing. I didn't even know what happened. And I panicked. But I found the tooth in the sink."

She was scrubbing her hair. The movements caused the towel around her body to unravel, sliding into a heap on her lap.

"And you were on the landing but the landing was different. It was like our landing but it was different 'cause it was up a flight of stairs. And I walked up. You were climbing a pair of ladders and I said, 'Annie, I didn't even feel it but my tooth is out'. And when I was speaking to you I started tasting blood in my mouth. I hadn't up to then. And I wiped my mouth and my hand was all blood. And you were raging. You went 'I don't want to talk to you just now'. And I could see you'd been crying so I walked back down the stairs and looked in the mirror at my tooth."

"You keep having dreams where I'm angry at you."

"I know. But it's strange about the tooth."

"Maybe you should go to the dentist."

"Maybe. It's a waste of money."

Her hair wasn't dry but she left it. She started to rub moisturiser up and down each arm then onto her stomach. I was watching as her body began to shine. Watching her breasts. But she never put the cream on her breasts.

"I've got that meeting today," I said.

She was looking in the mirrored wardrobes. Running a brush through her hair.

"What one is that again?"

"At the gallery. I'm meeting the woman who decides on what pieces they display from local artists."

"Oh, that's good then. What time?"

"No time really. She said to go in and have a chat whenever so I'm going to go down today."

She stopped brushing and turned on the hairdryer. The noise didn't help my head. She was ruffling her hand through and I watched the way the hair got stuck for a second in the spaces between her fingers. Thinking of how to capture that moment. What it'd look like. It wouldn't even take the shape of a woman. Of her. You could only really capture a moment like that in some other way. To do it justice. Her subtlety. Sometimes that was how ideas started. Other times you just painted and let it unfold. But more and more I was starting to think about doing other things. Things with everyday items. Like using Emulsion and seeing what I came up with. Just charge on in to B and Q and pick up a few pots of Dulux. Start going at a wall in the street.

It wasn't right how she kept fixing the towel back around her body.

The hairdryer overheated and turned off. She sighed then said, "Can you remember to do the washing. I need that dress for tomorrow night."

"That's fine. But can you send me a text later to remind me. Or an email."

"Why don't you do it soon so you don't forget? It'll have to be done soon so it'll be dry in time."

"Do you want it done now?"

"Well it doesn't have to be right now, but do it soon so you don't forget."

She stood and put her bra on. She'd left the towel on the bed and was naked except for the bra. She bent over to into her underwear drawer. She was bent over like that for a while. If a stranger had walked in it'd have looked like a seduction. Her for me. Using her body to tempt me.

"And can you wash pants for me too. I've hardly any pants. Can you wash the big ones. They're in the basket."

"Anything else?"

She was moving about the room now. The pants were on and she was getting make up and things. Pulling on skirts then taking them off again. Leaving them lying on the floor. Leaving them for another time.

"Just whatever else there is. What are you going to wear?"

"I've got that suit that my Dad brought round. I could wear that."

She stopped her routine and stared at me.

"Alex, it's navy. You can't wear navy. Everyone else will be wearing black."

"I've not got a black suit."

"Can't you borrow one from somebody?"

"Aye, that's what I'll do. I'll just go to the neighbours across the hall and go 'oh sorry to bother you Mrs, but can I borrow your black suit. I'm a 40-inch chest. Do you have that size? What? Just size 16? Okay then, I'll try that. No? Well, thanks anyway, cheerio!' That's what I'll do. Fuck sake."

"Don't speak to me like that. There's no reason for you to speak to me like that."

Annie sat down on the bed and turned the hairdryer back on. It clicked to go on but didn't work. She clicked it off and on a few times. She was sighing.

"Fuck sake," she said.

"I'm just a bit stressed," I said.

"Well so am I but I'm not taking it out on you."

"I didn't mean to get angry."

The hairdryer came alive and she finished with her hair. She straightened it and again I wondered how best to capture the way it struggled through her fingers.

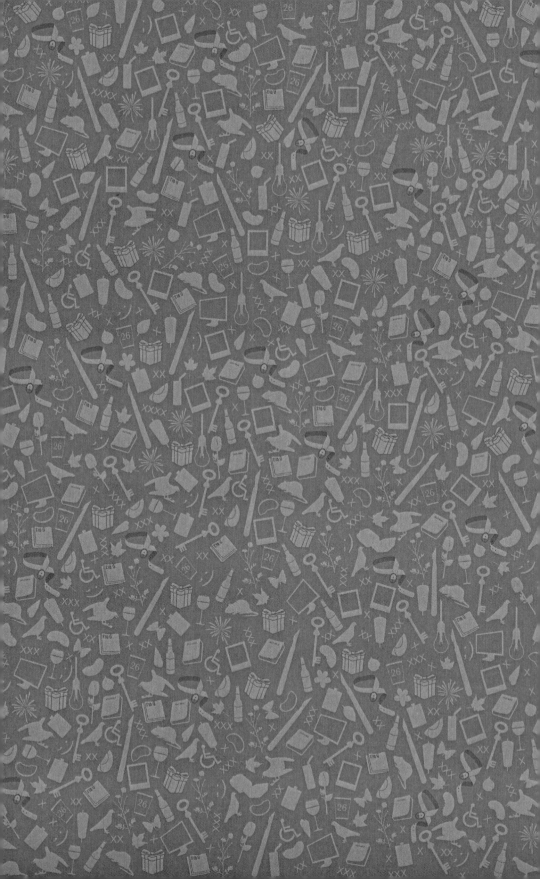

Her Last Night

She went back to flipping the burgers. She had three on the go and a short stack at the back corner of the hot plate. There were onions sizzling on the far side.

"I'll give you £1.90 but I want two burgers in the bun."

She looked beyond me. "It's too quiet tonight. The prices aren't negotiable."

"And those onions. I want some of those onions."

"It's £1.90 for a burger. One burger. You can have all the onions you want."

"It's no wonder you're shutting down then." I checked the onions. "I only like the burnt ones. I want them cremated."

"Sauce?" she said.

"No."

"Cheese?"

"Is it extra?"

She didn't answer. When she'd finished making my burger she wrapped it in a napkin and said, "Call it £1.90."

I gave her two pounds. "Keep the change."

The lights of the pubs and nightclubs were flashing in the distance. People were getting out of taxis and running to shelter from the rain. I heard the door at the back of her van open. She nodded as she approached. I noticed that her hair wasn't actually blonde. The way she'd pulled it back you could see grey roots growing an inch out her scalp.

She took a packet of fags from her apron pocket and knocked the bottom, making a few stick up.

"I'm trying to give up," I said.

"What's that?"

"My voice," I tapped my throat. "I'm trying to give up the fags."

"Hmm, me too," she said.

The smell of her cigarette was blowing into my face. I chewed my burger.

"See the fags are really bad for my voice. That's why I'm trying to give up."

"For your voice?"

"Just that they make it croaky. Sometimes I can't hit the high notes..." I finished what was in my mouth. "Twenty years I smoked."

She took a draw and swapped the cigarette to her other hand. She glanced up at me.

"I'm a singer," I said.

She turned to face me. She had the hand holding the fag up at her mouth and her other arm folded across her chest.

"What type of singer are you?"

"I get paid for it, if that's what you mean."

"I meant what type of stuff do you sing?"

"Can you not guess?" I pointed to my clothes.

She looked me up and down, "Christ... You're Elvis."

She kept staring. I took another bite.

"Where do you do that then?" she said.

"Had two jobs tonight actually. Well, one job and then after that this guy asked if I'd go back to his flat and do a private show for him and a few pals. It's good you know, getting work from the work."

"Can you sing like him?"

"That's not for me to say, is it?"

"You must know if you're good. You must be quite good if you're getting work."

I shrugged. I dipped into my carrier bag and brought out one of my records. "You be the judge."

She looked at the cover and stepped back. "Is this Elvis on the front?"

"Which one, me or him?"

"Did you use a professional photographer for it?"

I put the last of the burger in my mouth. "Few years ago now I got that done. I've put on a bit of weight this last while. Since I gave up the fags. Started walking home from gigs, trying to get fit again. Elvis wasn't skinny but. Not when he got to this age."

"What age is that then?"

"What age am I? Have a guess."

She looked at my face, my hair.

"Late thirties, early forties?"

"Aye, something like that," I said.

"You know, there actually is a wee bit of the Elvis look about you. About the mouth. You've got that mouth thing he had."

I finished chewing. "That's nice of you to say..."

"Liane."

"That's nice of you to say Liane. Thing is, this is the smile God gave me. No practice. I'm saving to get my teeth whitened. I might look like Elvis but I've not got his money. Not yet."

She tapped the fag ash and watched it float down. "You ever thought about doing X Factor?"

"Nah. You've just got to be at the right place at the right time. And know the right people. Jobs for the boys type of thing."

She finished her fag, bent down and twisted it into the ground. She flicked the butt under the van.

"I'll go and put it on the now. I've got a CD player."

"It's worth a try," I said.

She closed the door behind her, flicked some dials on her cooking equipment, added the burgers she'd been cooking to the pile at the back, then turned around to the stereo. She put the CD in and straight away my voice kicked in, then the guitar and the drums. She had it on really loud. And 'cause of that window where she served the food it was really something. She was clicking her fingers and nodding along to the music.

"You're good," she shouted.

I raised my voice above the level of the music. "That's the actual backing track that was on the Elvis Presley album. We just took out the vocals and I recorded my voice. But that's Elvis' band. The band he used in real life."

She turned the music down and walked over to the window. "What you saying?"

I told her again.

"You sound dead like him. You wouldn't know it wasn't him."

"Thanks. You can keep the album by the way. I've a few left."

She smiled.

"You know, this place would make a dead good studio." I stepped back, sized the thing up and continued. "It's the acoustics. Sounds like I'm listening in a submarine or something. All the sound that focuses."

"There you go," she said, knocking on the wall. "I knew this place had to be good for something." She paused for a few seconds and knocked on the wall again. It made a hollow dunt. "And it's sinking n all."

"Seriously," I said, "I'm getting an idea. I could record something in here. I've got equipment. It could be a real sweet sound. Authentic. Like they used to have. One mic hanging from the ceiling and me just playing. It'd be good to have a recording where I'm singing live."

"You serious?"

I slid my hands through the air. "I can see the title now, written in lights... Darren is... ELVIS LIVE!... That'd be a number one record by the way. I'll pay you."

She was watching me. "You're a dreamer," she said.

"You've got to be."

She turned the music back up a bit and I nodded along. It'd been a while since I'd heard the CD. She was right. I did sound like Elvis on it. Maybe the X Factor wasn't the worst idea. There's ten million Elvis impersonators. Even just to get my face known. Sing something so people will remember me.

"Any chance I could have one of your fags?" I said.

She turned the volume on the CD down a bit.

"Tut tut tut Elvis. And ruin that voice? I'll play no part in that."

I turned from her and looked up the street. It was busier now. Maybe if people came down to get a burger and heard my CD. Maybe some sort of record company exec, out on the town.

"You still hungry? You want another burger?"

"Nah, that's me skint."

"It's on me, for the..." she pointed her thumb towards the music.

"Aye well when you put it that way. Bit of a shame you're closing down now. I'm probably due a few."

She looked down at the grill. "Two burgers one bun? That do you?"

"Even better. I'd probably just have thrown that second bun away. You don't want too many carbs."

"Onions?"

"Lots of them."

"Cheese Elvis?"

She looked up then quickly looked past me.

I didn't know it was two boys at first. I thought maybe it was just a car passing by and leaving a shadow. Sometimes, especially up the town, you get a sense when there's somebody coming towards you. Normally on a work night I'm sober but now and again I'll take a drink. It's not good for the voice, but now and again it feels right. Sometimes a punter will buy you one. You hold the bottle up and some woman might shout "Cheers Elvis!"

"ThankyouMa'am."

And then you get a wee clap. Sometimes that's enough.

"Two hot dogs darlin," the boy at the front said. He was tall, skinny, the thighs at the front of his jeans as skinny at the top as they were at the bottom. His hair was in straggles. Long enough that it covered his ears or to be tied in a pony tail. He didn't look like the type who'd ever wear a pony tail.

I moved aside and let them in at the window. I leant with my back against the van.

"Two hot dogs for two hot dogs," Liane said.

"Oh she's a charmer int she? You're a charmer darlin," the one at the front said.

I could hear onions sizzling. I thought she must have put fresh ones on. Left the pre cooked ones on the back burner. There was a gap where the sealant had come away at the window. I could nearly see through but couldn't make anything out, just dark spots when she stepped between me and the light.

The smaller of the two men prodded his mate. "You hear that?" he pointed to the stereo. "Wee bit of Elvis. Canny beat a bit of the king eh? Here, they wee birds mate, shoulda been in there. What happened?"

"We should go to that club. Few more drinks and they'll be ours."

I stepped forward, put my hand on the shorter one's shoulder. He stopped speaking and turned quickly. I was touching him but it was Liane I spoke to. "You hear that? Your customers like the music."

She raised her eyebrows and nodded.

"They like Elvis. That's Elvis they're hearing right? Elvis."

"That's £3.00 for the two, boys," she said, "Are yous wantin juice?"

"What, is there something the matter wi Elvis mate?" the stocky one said.

"Em, naw, it's just... Liane, how can I say this without sounding like a..." I laughed a bit. "You know what I mean, how can I..."

The big guy goes, "Are we missing something here?" He looked between me and Liane. Looked at her then looked at me. Liane pointed at me and nodded.

"That's Elvis," she said.

I pointed at my trousers. I pointed at my bag. "Can't you tell?"

"Here Mark, get a fuckin load of this guy."

The skinny guy had his hand out and was plucking coins from it then handing them to Liane. She took the money then passed him the two hot dogs. He turned my way. "They won't miss you in the dark mate."

"Elvis, here's your burger too," Liane said.

The wee stocky guy snorted. "Is that right aye? Is that you singin?"

"Just something I do."

I stretched around him. I was on my tiptoes to take the burger, leaning into the van's window. I winked at Liane, indicated the boys and rolled my eyes.

The two boys were facing me. About a footstep away.

"You got all the gear mate?" the skinny one said. "You got the jacket to match your pants?"

"If Elvis had it then I've got it. The jacket, a rhinestone belt, silver sunglassess."

The skinny one spoke to Liane. "Aye but he hasny quite got the looks, eh doll?"

I heard her suck in air. "Now you, that's not nice," she said.

"Show us the jacket mate," the stocky guy said.

I looked at Liane. She was watching me. I reached into my carrier bag and got the jacket out. I unfolded it and held it up. "Over seventy jewels on this bad boy," I said.

The stocky guy took it off my hands. "Bad boy?"

"Be careful with it," I said.

He was bent over, his head down towards his knees and laughing. The cuffs were trailing along the pavement. "Aw mate, aw mate, that's a fucking disaster." He stood up again and held it against his chest. "Look at the fucking size of it man. And it's heavy as fuck. Here..." He threw it to the skinny guy, "You try it. It'll fit you."

"I'm not fucking wearing it!"

He held it out like it was dirty.

"Just wear it man, it'll be funny as fuck."

I walked towards him with my hand out. "Okay okay. I'll have it back now mate."

He held it away from me and looked to Liane. "Think I should?"

I didn't hear her reply.

"You can be the young Elvis to this guy's old Elvis," the stocky guy said.

"Aye! Fucking right! I'm sexy Elvis! Here..." He handed his hotdog to the stocky guy.

He slid his arms into the sleeves of my jacket and pulled it on. He pulled the collar up around his neck.

"Aw mate, that looks fuckin cracking!" The stocky guy said.

"You look handsome son," Liane said.

The stocky guy walked towards me. "Here mate, can you take a photo of us." He handed me a mobile phone then grabbed the skinny guy by the arm and pulled him into the light of the burger van. "You just press that button on the screen."

I nodded.

I was about to take the photograph and the stocky guy shouted, "Stop, stop, wait a minute. You got gel Elvis?"

"I use wax."

"Give us it and we can spike his hair up."

The stocky guy came over and went into my bag. The skinny guy slicked the wax through his hair until it shone. The straggles disappeared and the front was thick like a wave, sticking taut and upright, six inches in the air. He twirled a few strands with his fingers and curled them down his forehead.

"Oh yass mate, that's it now," his pal said. "And now, smile with a kink in your lip. That's it. And when he takes the photo make sure you smile and say Vegas!"

The two boys laughed.

"Here, you get in the photo too darling. Mon, come and get your photo taken with the king."

Liane hesitated a second and then went.

The three of them stood side by side. Elvis was in the middle with the stocky guy and Liane flanking him. He wrapped his arms around their shoulders and the three of them shouted 'Vegas' as I pressed the button and the camera flashed. Liane asked me to take another. She gave me her phone and got me to take one of Elvis kissing her cheek. She looked younger when she was laughing. She made me take another photograph with both boys kissing a cheek each. She kept saying how she couldn't believe this was her last night.

Later, when they'd gone, she stood alone and had me take photos of her outside the van. Just her and the van. She was trying to make jokes, shouting daft words as her image was taken.

Onions!

Burgers!

No cheese hen!

I got my jacket from where they'd left it on the counter. I wrapped it around Liane's shoulders like a shawl. She kept telling me to take more photos, and when I did, the jewels on the jacket sparkled. When the memory was full she took her phone and deleted the ones from the start then had me take more. I don't know how long we were there. People came to buy food but she'd shout at them to go away then tell me to take another photo.

Sometimes she'd shout freedom instead of cheese. Sometimes she'd shout Elvis. It got so I became expert. I was moving props to garner effects. I got her in all sorts of positions, frying onions, bending down and peering into the fridge, using the light to highlight her face. Then photos of just her hand. Her hand holding a spatula and flipping a burger. A close-up of the grease on her apron. Then one of her eye. The lens right up at her eyeball and the flash lighting the dark. And each time I filled the memory she'd ask me to delete them and start again.

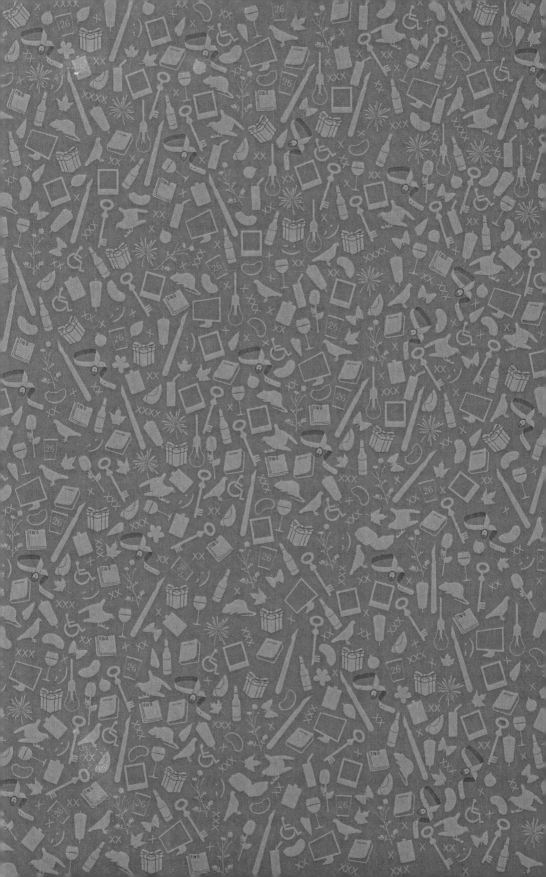

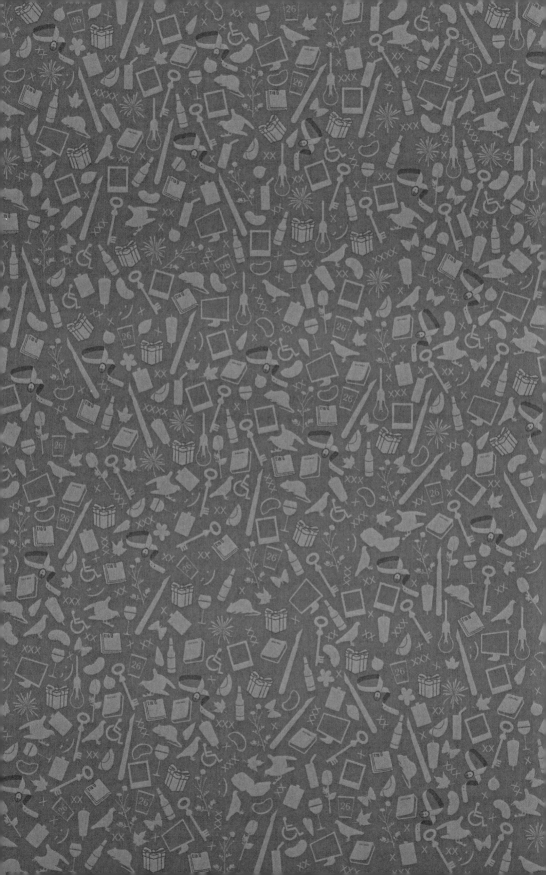

Boiler

The boiler guy, Marek she called him, had installed some kind of device that meant the gas travelled at a faster rate to her flat than anybody else's. But the problem was the noise. The boiler was hidden behind a pink gauze curtain in the corner recess in her bedroom. Chris asked her why there wasn't a door and she shrugged. Probably wasn't even her who'd put the curtain up. But the noise, Jesus. You'd be halfway into a dream and the thunder would start. A low drone for thirty seconds and then it kicked in. The gas throttling the pipes. You'd feel your whole body vibrate.

In the mornings she'd ask Chris how he slept, and sometimes the first thing he'd do was complain about the boiler: I'll never sleep in that room again. When you're out I'll make the living room the bedroom and the bedroom the living room. I'll get a hammer and murder it. Kasia would laugh and say something like, "But it sure is cosy, huh?"

In bed, the morning of the party, she suggested Chris invite a few friends.

"It's your flat as much as it is mine, isn't that what you think?" she said.

"It's you who asks me to stay most of the time."

She smirked.

"Well fine then," Chris said. "I'll invite a hundred friends if it makes you happy."

"Okay Chris. I can't wait to meet your," she tried to put on a deep Scottish accent, "hundred friends."

"My voice doesn't sound like that. I don't have that daft Polish twang, do I?"

She poked him in the ribs. "You mean beautiful accent."

"Hmmm, yeah. The way you build that catarrh at the back of your throat when you're speaking. It really is a thing of beauty."

"You should start to appreciate me," Kasia said.

She turned and faced the wall. Chris waited a minute. Kasia's hair looked different colours against the pillow and down her spine. Maybe being Polish made her skin that bit more delicate than his. It looked as thin as paper. Maybe it was just part of being female. He turned into her, raising his knees so they slid in behind hers. He kissed her neck.

"Is little baby Kasia in a huff puff?"

She shook her head.

He blew a raspberry on the back of her neck then put on a baby voice. "Yes she is, she is. Little Kasia is in a cream puff." He blew another raspberry until she pulled away.

"Stop. It tickles."

"Are you going to go out of your huff then?"

"No huff," she said.

"Are you going to go out of your huff?" He blew another raspberry.

She sighed then turned to face him.

"Okay, okay, God," she said. "Honestly, sometimes you are like a child."

"You're the one who went in a huff."

"I am tired, that is all."

It was Chris's shot to turn away now. He faced out the window. Every now and again the curtains moved with the draft.

They lay a while. She wouldn't speak. Kasia's breathing started to sound like sleep and Chris said, "It'll be that boiler waking you up all night. I don't think we should sleep with it on anymore."

She mumbled.

"I'm being serious. It's not just the noise. It dries the air as well. You wake up and you're parched. I'm needing glasses of water all day. It feels like a hangover."

"Maybe," she said, "but I like it warm."

He turned and cuddled in, lifting her neck and putting an arm under.

"Takes a while to get used to these Scottish winters eh?"

He began to kiss her neck.

"Do you think you could get used to this?" he said.

"I think maybe I could."

Chris moved his body in tighter to hers.

"What about this?"

"Later," she said. "I have to get up now."

He pulled his arm away and lay on his back, staring at the ceiling. Kasia slid the covers off and climbed over him. He put his hands on her hips and pressed her downwards.

"Nope," she said, "We can do it later."

"Twice later," he said.

"Maybe. But only after the party."

Chris listened as the boiler kicked in and the shower went on. For a while it just ran steady. The taps went on as she did the routine: wash the hands, wash the face, brush the teeth. Then the streams from the shower became inconsistent. Long gaps between the hiss from the shower head and the splashes on the base of the bath. Her body in-between. A loud wave as she rinsed out her hair.

She came back from the shower singing. A towel was wrapped around her body and another in a bun drying her hair. As she sang, she swung her head from side to side and the towel fell to the floor.

"Don't give up the day job," Chris said.

She went over to a suitcase in the corner and took out a hairbrush. She raised it to her mouth like a microphone then moved up to his face.

"I guess it will be me handling the music for the party then? We can't subject people to that type of thing."

She stopped singing and covered her mouth.

"Oh my God, I have no stereo."

"It's cool, I'll get one," he said.

"And chairs? Will we need chairs?"

"Relax, we'll get some. It's fine."

She shook her head.

"How many people are coming?" he asked.

"I don't know, twenty? Thirty? Fifty maybe?"

"Fifty? Fuck sake man, what if there's a fire?"

"Don't Chris."

He held the back of her neck. "It's okay," he said, "I'll sort it."

"I don't know," she said.

Kasia started getting ready and he watched her. How she moved around naked

like that. As if her body was just a body. Walking naked in front of him not caring
that he could see. She always made an effort. The make-up, her hair. Vaseline on
the lips. That routine. Maybe if he closed his eyes and looked for the memory hard
enough she'd be there, walking naked like that, singing to herself words he couldn't
understand. The drips at the end of the strands of her hair. Her little toes, curled
up against the cold. The way her nipples were hard because of it. The way her
lip petted as she searched for clothes that weren't where she thought they were.
The smile to herself, not witnessed by anyone anywhere but him, when she found
them. He closed his eyes to try and see it just right in his mind. Couldn't make it
last any longer than an instant.

The smiles of old girlfriends, could he remember them? He could see their faces
but not a smile specifically. Christ, had they ever smiled at him? The right thing to
do with Kasia would be to grab her by her shoulders and shake her before he could
dig his way in any deeper.

She kissed him before she went to work. He promised he'd get everything ready
for the party. Not to stress. To leave it all to him.

"I love you," she said.

She put on her coat, scarf and gloves. She kissed him again and left.

You only noticed the cold when you got out of the shower. Drops of water were static
on the hairs that stood upright from your hands. Chris walked over to the window
in the bedroom. There was a whistle as the air came in. He closed the curtains.

In the hallway there was another draft coming from the front door. It felt like
standing bare-legged in front of a fridge. This wouldn't do. Fair do's it was the first
week and that, but this was a bought home.

He twisted the towel into a thin strip, laying it between the door and the
laminate. It was impossible to gauge the success of this strategy in only a minute.
Naked and shivering he went back to the bedroom.

Even the floorboards were freezing. It was sore to stand still. Clothes might
help. Turn the boiler on full. He hopped to the pink curtain and flung it aside.
Right, let's see here. There were switches and dials and lights. In the bottom
corner a plug socket. He switched it off then on again. The boiler came to life,
the wild roar of it kicking in, but then a red light came on and it died. He tried
again and the same thing happened. He smacked the side of the boiler a few
times but nothing.

When Marek arrived he wasn't some bronzed Adonis; six foot three with a skin-tight
white t-shirt. If you didn't hear him speak he could easily have been Scottish.

He had that Celtic look about him, light skin and grey eyes. A bit of a pudge around the waist.

Marek smiled and shook Chris's hand.

"Marek," he said and pointed at himself. "You are?"

"I'm Chris."

"Okay good. Now come man and I'll show you."

Marek led the way to the bedroom.

"This type of thing man you know, it's common. I show you."

"I tried fiddling with it but no joy mate," Chris said. Then he added, "I think it might have something to do with what you did to it. It's really loud. Louder than it should be."

Marek shook his head. "No. I know what it will be. These are good boilers, the best. But no brand name. There is a factory that make these boilers and then they send them out to the companies who put labels on then double the price you know."

Marek slid the curtain aside. He looked at the boiler and held his chin.

"Did you do anything to it?"

"Not really."

"You didn't press this button?"

"I don't think so."

"Here?"

He pointed to the plug.

"I might have. But only to try and fix it."

Marek sighed and held his forehead.

"It wasn't working. I tried to fix it."

"Okay okay. Now in the future do not do this. It resets the electronics. If you have to turn it off then turn it off here okay?" He pointed at a dial on the centre of the boiler.

"Aye, cool. No problem."

"Okay, okay. Now..." he was rubbing his hands together. "This switch here, do you see it?"

Chris moved closer.

"If you ever see this light go from green to red then it is this switch which will fix it okay. This switch you turn this way and wait five seconds. Not less than five seconds. After five seconds you turn it back and..."

Marek turned the dial back to where it was and the light went green. A second later the boiler fired up and this time it did what it used to do. That growl then the floor shook beneath their feet. Marek stepped back and admired his creation.

"Okay? You understand?"

"Aye. Five seconds."

"This is a great boiler," he said. "The girl who lives here made a good choice with this one. It will last years. And remember, five seconds then switch. Then all better."

"Aye, thanks," Chris said.

Chris started to blow into his hands. Marek brushed past him and into the hall. He brought out a pad of paper from his overalls. He wrote down the details and held the receipt out towards Chris.

"You kiddin me on?" Chris said.

"It is a minimum charge of thirty minutes."

"But you were only here two."

Marek was waving the piece of paper about.

"Yes but it is minimum thirty minutes, do you understand? Minimum thirty minutes for a call out."

"But all you did was switch the thing on and off."

Marek let out a sigh and shook his head.

"This is a call out. You pay for my time. My time. Not for what I do. Okay?"

"Naw, it's not okay." Chris put his hands in his pockets and paced between the bedroom and the hallway. "You're ripping me off man. This isn't how people do things around here . You do people favours. You don't charge thirty quid for turning a fucking dial."

"Well you speak to my boss then. You explain this to him not me."

He started mumbling in Polish. Chris knew some of the swear words from Kasia. Marek was calling him a fucking this and a fucking that. He got his mobile out his pocket and began to make a call. Chris waited. You could see Marek's hands beginning to shake pressing the buttons.

Marek's boss said he should have been charging Chris for wasting his time on the phone call. Did Chris think he was better than other people? Everybody has to pay for at least a half hour. It's industry policy. Did he really think he was so special he didn't have to pay? You weren't paying for what the engineer actually did, you were paying for his time. His time, his time, his time. Like he could be curing cancer or painting a fucking masterpiece with his time.

Chris told Marek that if he was paying him for thirty minutes then he could earn his money. Fix the boiler back to normal. Get rid of the turbo charger he'd installed and stop it making that fucking din.

"And is that what the lady wants?" Marek said.

"She wants what I want."

"I take money first."

Chris put his hands on his hips and laughed. "Unbelievable man. You're going to have to change your manners if you want to keep living in this country."

Marek held his hand out. "Money now or I go and you deal with my boss."

"Aye okay. You can have your precious half hour's pay. You think I care about that? Spare change to me mate."

Chris went through his wallet and took out a twenty and a few pounds or so in change. There was some shrapnel in Kasia's suitcase that got added to the kitty.

Marek took the money and dug it into the pocket of his overalls.

Chris pointed him in the direction of the bedroom and repeated exactly what he wanted. A normal boiler. No fancy engineering. Something that didn't make you think the house was falling down.

Chris went through to the living room and sat on the floor. He made a list of the things he had to do. Get chairs, find stereo, invite friends. He stood up. Outside it was getting dark. He scratched at the frost on the glass.

"Are you not finished yet man?" he shouted.

There was no reply.

"Can't believe you're not finished man. That is truly shocking. And you call yourself a professional?"

When thirty minutes were up Marek came out, slapping his hands together and coating the laminate in dirt.

"So?" Chris said.

"There are problems you know. Some problems with the boiler. You have done something to it."

"I've not done anything mate. It's you who has done something to it."

He shook his head. "You give me more money and I'll fix it," he said. "Another thirty minutes. Maybe more."

"Get to fuck man, just fucking forget it." Chris went forward and opened the door. "Give me back my money."

"No."

Chris clenched his fists.

"You are paying me for my time. Thirty minutes I stay. So you pay."

Chris pressed his thumb deep into his cheek and cocked his head to the side. "You know what man, you're so pathetic that I don't even care. You can keep it. You're scum, you know that? Immigrant scum. You even legal man?"

Marek sneered at Chris. He packed up his gear and pushed past out to the landing. "I will come back when the lady is in I think. She was much more welcoming. A very friendly girl."

Marek drew his fingers together, lifted them to his lips and licked them.

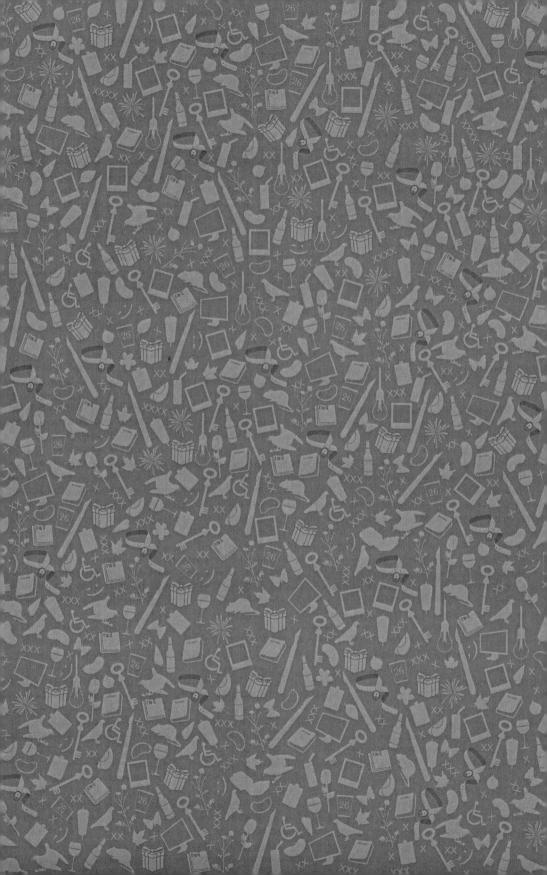

Rats

Cullen said we should get a game of darts at Steiny's until the rain went off.
I said I'd spoken to him earlier and he was away to Glasgow Green with his
family for the big display. Cullen said we should crack a window and climb in
anyway. Get a game then get out. Mark said it was the best idea he'd heard all
day. Cullen said he needed a shite. He went down a lane and we waited on him.

He washed his hands in a puddle then flicked the water at me and Mark.

"Kebab shop?" he said.

It was one of those three-in-one places that did curries and pizzas as well.
The guy that worked there would say, "One ned at a time please. Don't you see
the sign?" There was no sign.

"Yous think Glasgow Spice will be working tonight?" Mark said.

Cullen said, "Hate that guy, man. He thinks he's mental."

"What about the woman?" Mark said. "Hiding her face behind that fucking
cloak. She's worse."

"My Dad calls her a peek-a-boo Mama," I said.

"Stupid boot," Cullen said.

Mark started to do the accent and was going, "Veek-a-voo Mama!
Shish kebab vor Veek-a-voo Mama!"

I was glad I'd told the lie about Steiny. He was different these days. He said he couldn't hang about with Cullen anymore 'cause he didn't trust himself not to start a scrap. He had a new girlfriend I hadn't met but he'd been seeing her for two months. My Mum says sometimes friends lose touch.

At the three-in-one Cullen ordered first. "Shish Kebab mate. Name's Willy."

Me and Mark were at the doorway trying to get warm. You could steal the heat coming from the donner on the skewer. If you looked quickly you could see where the chef fired up the naan bread as the door swung open and shut. When the door closed it had a window that looked like a mirror with gaps. I put my hands out as if the shop was a fire. Mark leant over my shoulder and shouted "Villy Vonka! Shish kebab vor Villy Vonka!" then bolted out of sight leaving me standing like that in the doorway.

It was the young guy that everyone called Glasgow Spice who was working. He had a shaved head with a pattern stencilled in the side. He looked at me.

"Think you're funny wee man?" he said.

Cullen went, "I am truly, truly sorry," then turned to me and wagged his finger. "Jamie! For goodness sake. You are such a racist young man. Show some respect, Jamie."

I walked out the doorway to the street. Mark had done the off and for a minute I was alone. Fireworks lit up the sky in blues and greens. I took my finger and drew my name in the sky. Wondered if you could get fireworks to spell out your name. How for a second it'd light up a hundred feet high. People all across the city would know your name. How much would that cost? Steiny could do it for his bird. Write her name in the sky.

Cullen clicked his fingers in front of my eyes. "You're next, baw jaws. Glasgow Spice says you're a wee wank. Hunner quid if you smash his jaw."

"Maybe," I said.

I went in and says to the guy, "Small shish mate."

He mumbled something to me in his language then shouted through to the back. The old chef came out, wiping his hands on his apron. The young guy went and said something in his language again and pointed at me. The chef started to laugh. He was shaking his head at the young guy. As he went back to the kitchen I saw his grin in the reflection from the door. You could still hear him laughing when it swung shut.

"A small shish you're wanting aye?" the young guy said.

"That's right."

"Seven pound forty."

"Seven forty? It's never seven forty!"

He laughed, shouted through the back again then turned to me. "I'm just kidding you wee man. Three pound forty."

He held out his palm and I gave him the exact change.

He laughed again. "Nae bother wee man. Small shish it is." He shouted through to the back again and you heard the old chef's laughter louder than any of the fireworks outside.

The young guy leaned forward on the counter and almost whispered to me. "So what are the young team doing the night then?"

"Us? Nothing. Just watching the fireworks."

"Is that it aye?" He was nodding fast.

I looked past him at the posters on the wall. There was a picture of the Taj Mahal or Mecca or something and one of those little snap off month calendars that they give you in school when you're making a present for your Mum at Christmas.

"Not causin trouble then?" he said.

I glanced at him. "Not us mate."

He turned away and began to carve meat from the donner into a metal tray. He sang as he worked. Some song I couldn't understand.

"Think I'm a good singer wee man? You like it?"

When I didn't answer he laughed and said, "Tunak Tunak Tun, wee man. Tunak Tunak Tun."

There was a copy of *The Sun* on the counter. I picked it up then sat on a stool to wait.

"You know wee man, I love my job. I really do," the guy said.

I read every story in the sport section. All the time the guy was jumping about dancing and singing. I poked my head out of the door. Pissing down. There were still a lot of fireworks in the distance but you couldn't hear them much. Mark and Cullen weren't about. I stepped out to see if they were in a doorway but it was perishing. There were only so many places they could be. It was getting late. I could just head home with the kebab. Lie in bed and stay awake until my feet got warm. Put on fresh socks. Eat my kebab in bed.

When I got back both guys were through the back kitchen and even though the door beeped when I went in Glasgow Spice never came through.

An old drunk came in. He was staggering. He came in and slumped down on the empty stool beside me. "Awright pal," he said.

Glasgow Spice came back through. He went, "Davie ya maddy, what can I do you for the night ma man?"

The drunk made his way forward. He pointed at the menu that was taped to the countertop.

"A mixed grill Davie? You sure?"

The drunk nodded.

"That's no cheap Davie."

The drunk opened and closed his mouth. The saliva clogged together so that you could hear it. "Don't you worry about Davie son..." he shook his pocket. It jingled like there were a thousand coins in it.

"Puggy?" the Asian guy went, but the drunk just tapped his nose then came and sat back on the stool next to me.

Glasgow Spice went back through to the kitchen. I kept flicking through the paper. I wasn't even reading it. The old drunk was swaying from side to side, brushing against me and stinking of pish.

I stood again and went to the door. I ran along the street for a while to try and find them. I sheltered under the cover at the cafe and looked in through the gaps between the shutters. I could see the green light from the cash register at the far side and the glow from the fly killer lit the tables up in blue.

On my way back to the three-in-one the old drunk was eating his tandoori sausage like it was a banana. I ran past him and back in to the shop. Glasgow Spice was through the back again. I saw him peek at me through the gaps in the mirror. I went to the door and opened it then shut it so the beep would come on. When he never came I rapped on the counter with my knuckles. "Hello," I shouted. "Here, can I get my food?"

I sat back down on the stool. Picked up the paper then stood again. "Hello? Can I get some service here?"

I went to the door. Open, shut. Open, shut. Made it beep five times. It was only when I went and lifted the counter top, lifted it up and over then went to walk through the kitchen that he came out.

"What you playing at? Staff only."

I stepped back. "Twenty minutes I've been waiting here man."

He held a finger in the air to shoosh me. He called through to the back kitchen. The old chef came out. The young guy spoke in English. "Have you made this gentleman a shish kebab?"

The chef put his hands out and shrugged.

"I says a shish kebab? Have. You. Made. A. Shish. Ke. Bab?"

The chef shrugged again.

Glasgow Spice turned to me. "He doesny understand me wee man. You try asking him."

I could feel myself beginning to shake.

"Go on wee man. You ask him if he has made you a shish kebab."

"Did you?" I said, staring at the chef.

The chef looked to the young guy.

"I says did you make my kebab?"

Glasgow Spice nodded his head, indicating me. "Kabob?" he said.

The chef shrugged. "Kabob?" he said. "No. No kabob."

Glasgow Spice gasped, put his hands to his cheeks then said, "No kabob?"

"No fucking kebab? Fuck sake man. Twenty fucking minutes I've been waiting."

"Oh sorry sir. See, we're stupid here. People from our country are a wee bit slow. We don't understand sometimes you know."

I threw the paper on the floor.

"This is a disgrace. You think that's right? I paid yous man."

"Sorry sir. We no understand what you're saying. Maybe if you speak more slowly?"

He was exaggerating his accent. Glasgow was gone. He held his hands out in front of him, palm to palm as if in prayer.

"We no understand the western gentleman."

"Everyone is right about you. Yous are just scam artists. Fucking terrorist paki bastards. That's what you are."

"I am sorry sir. Me do not understand."

"Understand this?"

I raised my middle finger in the air. Kicked the stool over and it rattled against the wall. When I walked outside I never even felt the cold. I looked through the window at them. Glasgow Spice was pointing at me and shouting "Mon then wee man! Come ahead." He began to laugh.

The old chef fixed the stool then made his way back through the kitchen door. The young guy kept staring at me, hands out by his side.

"You come out here ya dick," I said. "I'll take you out here."

He lifted the countertop and made his way towards me. But there was two of them and just me so I ran to find Cullen and Mark. Get the fireworks from Cullen and blow their whole fucking shop up. Get a rocket and fire it at the red dot he should have had painted between his eyes.

On the ground was the carton old Davie had been carrying. There was a pile of meat in a puddle of rain. I booted it into the air. "Cullen! Mark!"

I went up to the canal. The water was rushing along at a thousand miles per hour. I ran to the bushes where we sometimes sat. I passed through the tunnel where we'd get a drink under. "Cullen...Mark..." Then I ran further on. Up to where the lock was. Where the water bubbled up rank and we'd sat in the summer dangling our legs over and fishing. I stopped to catch my breath. My skin was damp. Then in the distance I saw a spark. I saw the fuse take light and there was a bang so loud that birds went flying from trees. I was under the tunnel and the sound felt like it came in, got trapped for a few seconds, and went out the other side.

When the noise stopped there was a ringing in my ear but I could make out laughter in the distance. I started towards them, "Cullen... Mark!" A slow jog and just as I was about to break into a run I noticed them. All those rats being swept downstream. Their heads just above the water as they escaped whatever it was Mark and Cullen had done.

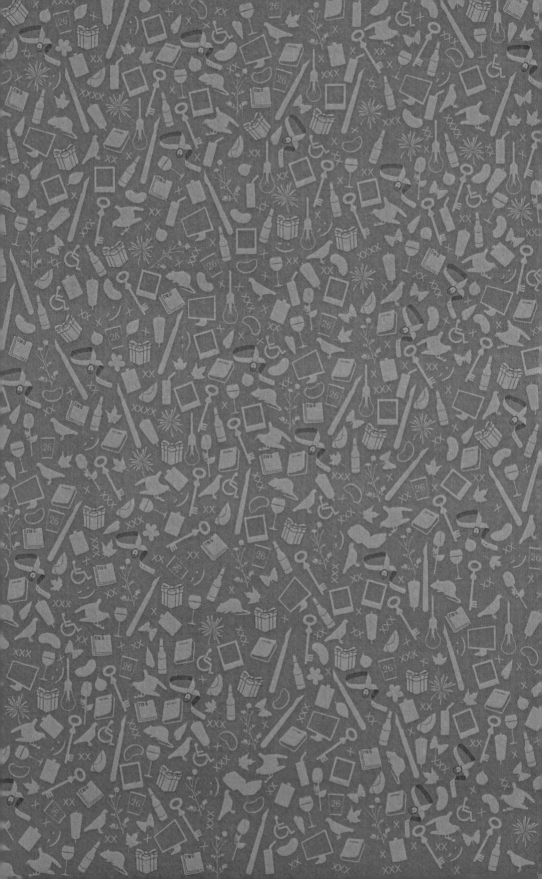

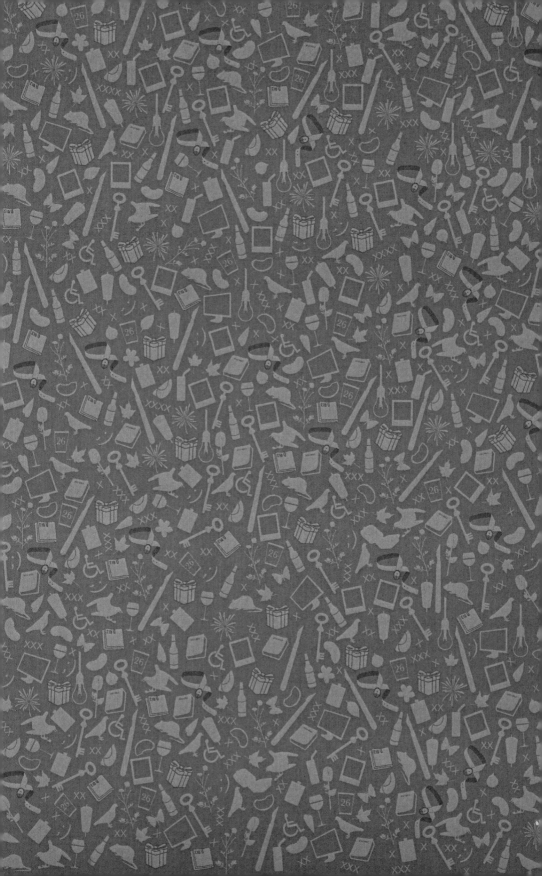

Sharkman #1

Jimmy was my boss but he'd sit with me at lunch. He'd seen me reading my book once and I guess that gave him the idea. I must have been twenty-one or twenty-two at the time and carried a copy of Young Adam around hoping someone would notice me. I'd walk Byres Road end-to-end with it sticking half out the back pocket of my jeans.

I must have read that first chapter a thousand times. It was always that first chapter, where Trocchi has Joe look in the mirror and say the 'I' standing before him is not the 'I' which is the self. That the problem is the words. The language. That we can never see the truth because of it. Joe fishes a naked woman's body out of the canal. Her skin white as paper. He has breakfast and Ella lies to him about there being no eggs. He sees the remains of the yolk dripping yellow between the prongs of her fork.

I don't know who I expected to notice me. You heard stories about Alasdair Gray being spotted in the pubs, painting the walls in return for free drinks. You heard Stuart Murdoch from Belle and Sebastian could usually be found in a coffee shop. What I am sure of is that I never imagined the person to notice me to be like Jimmy.

Jimmy's five year plan was to be retired from Supermarket management and tour the world with his comic book. He told me everything you'd ever want to know about his superhero – date of birth, where he went to school, shoe size, favourite breakfast cereal, everything. A lot of it was based on Jimmy and at first I never understood how it'd work.

"So you're telling me he's half and half? Like both at once? Does he mutate or something?"

"Mutate? God, no. It's a genetic experimentation gone wrong. The crux is this... He can't predict when it will happen. Not at first anyway. He has to learn how to control his power. You know the whole 'with great power comes great responsibility' mantra."

"I think so," I said.

Jimmy sighed. "Look, think about it. What have Batman, Spiderman and Catwoman all got in common?"

I shrugged. "Costumes?"

"Animals."

"Animals?"

"Animals. But spiders? Cats? Bats? Do me a favour. What the world needs is a real superhero. Something dangerous."

"Spiders are deadly mate."

"Are you kidding me? If a tarantula tried to bite me I'd pull its legs off. You ever seen a tarantula up close? I have. They're smaller than your hand my friend. But a shark..."

"Okay, okay," I said, "but what's the story? You need a story. Like how Peter Parker was bitten by a spider and that gave him powers. What's the..."

When Jimmy wanted you to finish speaking he'd wind his hand until you stopped.

"What's the deal with the shark guy?"

"Sharkman."

"Aye, Sharkman."

Jimmy had a quick glance round the canteen then leant in close.

"Well... His name is Johnny Smith. Get it? John Smith. Sharkman is all of us."

I nodded.

"Johnny is just a normal guy. He's thirty six and works as a waiter. He's always worked as a waiter. Thing is though, he's started a new job in a fancy restaurant. But the restaurant is in a government facility and there's a department there called the Centre for Aquatic and Subterranean Habitats." Jimmy looked up at me, "or CASH."

"Cool," I said.

"Big time. So one day a scientist from CASH, a professor named Merman Helville..."

"Named what?"

Jimmy raised his hand.

"...named Merman Helville. He requests that his meal be delivered to his laboratory. He doesn't want to leave because he thinks he's making a career-defining breakthrough. But here's the rub – Johnny is assigned to take the meal down. When the scientist sees him, he's so deluded from lack of sleep and shark experimentation that he ignores the food and notices that Johnny is six foot one and a half - the exact same height as the beast he's been working on. There's only one way he'll ever fully be able to read that shark's thoughts."

Jimmy smiled and tapped the side of his temple with his finger. Barry, one of the other bosses, walked into the canteen. Jimmy spotted him, looked at me, then rolled his eyes. They chatted about work stuff until it was time for Jimmy and me to get back to the shop floor. He filled me in on the way upstairs.

"Johnny's skin develops gills. And his eyes, they turn black like shark eyes. They're the sign when he's turning. They go vacant and when someone looks into them and it's like looking into the void. When that happens he only has minutes to get to water."

By the time Jimmy finished we were in the chill where the stock was kept.

"You're on yoghurts," Jimmy said. "Get a move on."

Working in the supermarket wasn't a bad job, but most of the time they put me on the 12-10. You have a pretty eventless life doing the 12-10. No time to do anything worthwhile in the morning and no time to do much of use after finishing. Normally I'd just get a few drinks with the other late finishers then stagger home at chucking out time.

A lot of times when I was working I'd catch myself thinking about Jimmy's Sharkman. I remember wondering whether he would only be able to fight crime out at sea. About whether or not he'd have a suit. The thing with Jimmy was that unless we were talking about Sharkman or the books I was reading we'd only talk about work. Had I seen the mess in Home and Leisure? What the hell were clothing up to with their displays? What could I do personally to cut our waste? Out of all the departments people said that we had it toughest. We had to face-up non-stop. Plus Jimmy wanted the chill as sparkling as the aisles. If there was a spill in the aisles and we hadn't started cleaning it before the cleaners arrived then Jesus, he'd take you out the back and go through you like wind.

If the department was looking good Jimmy would send us somewhere else –

Produce to stock the carrots; Beers, Wine and Spirits to count the bottles. Even the aisles with the stinking fish. Face things up. Make sure you rotate. Oldest to the front. Reduce things nearly out of date. All that stuff. Jimmy demanded it. People would ask me how I could sit with him at lunchtimes, how could I even look the bastard in the eye.

A couple of times Jimmy asked me to have lunch in his car. It was one of those family people carriers. The back seat had headphones and DVD cases lying about it. There were empty crisp packets and chocolate wrappers. He swept a lot of shit off the passenger seat so I could sit down.

He kept all of his stuff in one of those big canvas IKEA bags. Piles of loose leaf sheets filled top to bottom with script, full coloured sketches of Sharkman, close-ups of a fin emblazoned with an S.

"Sharkman!" Jimmy said.

"Holy shit Jimmy, this is a life's work."

"Nah, just fifteen years on and off," he said.

I went through the pages. There wasn't any order, just screeds of writing, storyboards, mock comic strips and lists of character names. He'd even written obituaries.

"Look here," Jimmy said. "In human form Johnny Smith still has very sharp teeth, see?"

Jimmy talked me through the sketches.

There was a half idea for a sidekick who Jimmy called Sharkboy. This kid had gone swimming and started struggling in the currents too far out. He was drowning when Sharkman saw him. He died in Sharkman's arms. But Sharkman wouldn't leave it. He ended up begging to the deep for this kid's life and somehow the thing that gave him his power got transferred to this boy. It meant they were linked for life. When Sharkboy felt pain, Sharkman felt pain. There was a nemesis too, a spirit that could take on any form, simply called 'The Being'. And there was a love interest, I think, but I can't remember anything about her.

"I was going to ask you a favour," Jimmy said.

"Okay mate, sure."

"I'm planning on turning a lot of this into a film script but I'm not the best with computers. And you've got that degree. Thought you might be able to help with how to do the script, layout and things, spelling."

"I'll have a think," I said. "Give me one of the pages and I'll try and do something with it then you can see how it looks."

"You don't mind?"

"No problem mate, it'll be easy."

Jimmy handed me the whole bag.

"I don't need it all, just give me a few sheets."

"Here, just take it. Choose whatever you want. Anything you can do."

"Only if you're sure."

"Yeah, yeah, absolutely. I'll give you a lift home with it later."

"I could maybe scan a few of the images in for you as well, if you want."

"Wow, yeah. Anything. That would be fantastic."

It took a week or so to type up the work. I made up a template on Word with boxes down the left hand side where he could write the name of the character speaking. The way I'd done it meant that when he wrote the name it'd automatically turn to bold and Caps. I'd put in space for stage direction that would automatically turn to italics. I suppose the way I done it was more like a play than a film but that was all I knew.

Jimmy gave me his email address and I sent through the file. I wrote that when I got a chance I'd do a bit more. That I'd try and put a little mock comic strip together just so he could see what it'd be like. I got a picture of Jaws and sent it as an email attachment to make him laugh.

It was round about then that Jimmy's daughter Erin started in the work. She was on some school work experience thing and was meant to go to a newspaper. Erin told me that when she grew up she wanted to be a journalist. When the newspaper job fell through Jimmy managed to get her into the supermarket. He asked me if it was okay for her to pair up with me. The word he used was mentor – could I be her mentor.

I more or less used Erin to half my workload. She was enthusiastic about the place the way only a fifteen year old could be. If she was pretending not to notice the attention she was getting from the boys then she was playing coy better than girls twice her age. She had inherited Jimmy's height, must have been pushing 5'11 and was slim as a rail. But she wasn't really my type and plus, she was Jimmy's daughter.

The problem wasn't that the boys said she was cute or pretty or had potential. There were no euphemisms. What they said was how come I was the lucky fucker that got to look after her? That sexy piece of jailbait ass. You can't buy pussy that prime. Keeping Erin away from them was the hardest job I've ever had. If Jimmy was about they'd stay back but if he was off the shop floor they'd bat me away to get to her. Some of these guys were going for the kill, trying to get her number, taking photos on their phones when she was bent over, timing their breaks with hers. Honestly man, whatever it is that people want, Erin had it.

I decided to talk to Jimmy about it. Told him that what I was going to say was in confidence and I was only telling him because he deserved the truth. He went really quiet when I told him. As if he'd never imagined she could be attractive before.

Back upstairs he told her to go through to the chill. I'd been on the end of a verbal from Jimmy a few times and though it was never a good pace to be, it had nothing on what Erin was going through. You could hear him from the shop floor; not words but the sound of him, tonal, tribal, his anger going through the girl. When customers began looking down the staff only entrance I had to go in. The shouting got louder as I walked along. By the time I opened the door I'd broken into a run. Jimmy had her pressed tight against the chill wall.

"That's enough!" I shouted.

They turned to me. Erin's eye liner had run and spread across her cheeks.

"Leave her Jimmy."

"Leave her?" he said.

"She can't help it," I said.

Everything about Jimmy was different then. The way his fingers were bent in on themselves, the way he shrouded over her like that, spit down his chin.

"The customers mate, they'll hear you."

He stared at Erin for a few seconds then stepped back and looked at the floor.

"Pack up your stuff and go home," he said.

Erin was sobbing as she ran past me. Then it was just me and Jimmy.

"You okay?" I said.

"Did customers complain?"

"I'm sorry mate," I said.

"Fuck," he said and gripped his hair, "fuck, fuck, fuck, fuck, fuck."

"Just calm down mate, it'll be okay."

He started pacing up and down the chill.

"I just lost it, you know. The red mist. I don't remember."

He was taking deep breaths then exhaling.

"Will I go and see if she's okay?" I said.

"No, leave it. I'll go."

When he left I started cleaning up a box of eggs that had fallen during the fight. A few of them had broken and I wiped up the slime and pieces of shell then binned them.

For a few weeks after that I didn't see much of Jimmy. He'd started taking his lunches at different times. Sometimes I'd think of going over but whenever he caught me looking I'd turn away and get back to work.

Erin got in touch during that time. Said she'd got my number from her

Dad's phone. All the text messages were about how she was so mortified. But thanks so much for helping her. I got back and told her if she ever needed a reference then I'd give her one no problem. There were always kisses at the end of her texts: 'Thanks babe xxxxx', 'Do you wanna meet up for coffee or something sometime babe? xxxx' I only wrote things that could be read innocently.

Sometimes she'd text when it had nothing to do with anything. 'What you doing? I'm bored! LOL xxx' I wondered if three kisses like that – xxx, meant sex. I'd stay up sometimes and text her into the night. We arranged to meet up after the New Year. She had her prelim exams and her birthday in December. She said if I could wait until January she'd make it worth my while. 'Don't tell my Dickhead Dad xxx'

It wasn't until just before the Christmas night out that Jimmy and I spoke again. He asked me to go into the chill so he could have a word.

"Are you going tomorrow night?" he said.

"Aye, it should be good. Are you?"

Jimmy glanced about.

"You want to meet beforehand? Grab a beer then head down together?"

"I've already arranged to meet some of the boys," I said.

"Oh... Right. I was thinking you could give my stuff back to me."

"I mean I'm sure you could come, I'm sure it'd be alright with everyone."

"Nah, they won't want to be seen drinking with one of the bosses."

"Don't be stupid mate, it won't be..."

"Look, tell you what, bring the bag and I'll get it at the night out. I've booked a room at the hotel anyway so what to do is I'll give you a call or a text with the room number and you can bring the bag up when you get there."

"Aye man, fine. Look mate, I've not really had the time to get much of it onto the computer. Just with work and whatever else. But I'll bring what I've done."

"Been too busy have you?" he said.

"Aye mate, kind of. Sorry."

Jimmy stepped back, nodded his head at one of the milk cages, then started to walk off.

I went back to work.

I turned up to the night out with the Sharkman papers in carrier bags within the IKEA bag. I did my best to keep it away from the boys but after a few beers I showed them. Someone laughed so much he said he'd pissed his pants. After that all they ever called Jimmy was Sharkman. They made up a theme tune.

When we got to the hotel nobody had seen Jimmy so I checked the bag into the cloakroom. There was an Elvis tribute act playing and this checkout girl Lynne got caught shagging him in the toilets. When he came back out for the second half somebody shouted, "Elvis, gonnae play Love me Tender." "Aye, or Jailhouse Cock," someone else said.

It was later on, in the gents, when I met Jimmy. I'd been texting Erin, begging her to sneak out and come down. I told her I'd book a room, scatter rose petals on the bed and get us a bucket load of champagne. I was halfway through my piss when I felt his hands on my shoulders.

"Did you bring my stuff?" he said.

I turned quickly and dripped down the front of my jeans.

"Jimmy fuck sake, I'm kinda busy here."

He moved his hand onto my neck and pressed my face up against the bathroom wall.

"Where's my Sharkman stuff?" he said, "Do you think I'm an idiot or something?"

"It's in the cloakroom mate. I left it in the cloakroom."

"You're not answering my question."

I wriggled to get free but Jimmy held me tight.

"You miss me, don't you" he said.

"What?"

"You can admit it."

I tried to turn again but Jimmy tightened his grip.

"Say it," he said.

His breath was warm on the back of my head.

"You're hurting me," I said.

"You never think you're hurting me?"

"Jimmy, stop it man."

He moved in closer.

"Say it then. Say you miss me."

"Jimmy..."

"Say it."

My voice started to break.

"I miss you man," I said, "I miss you so much."

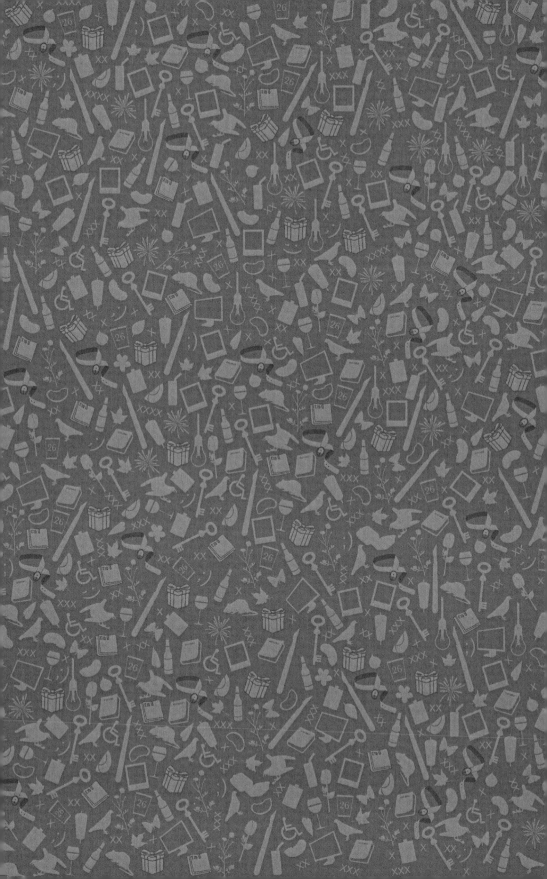

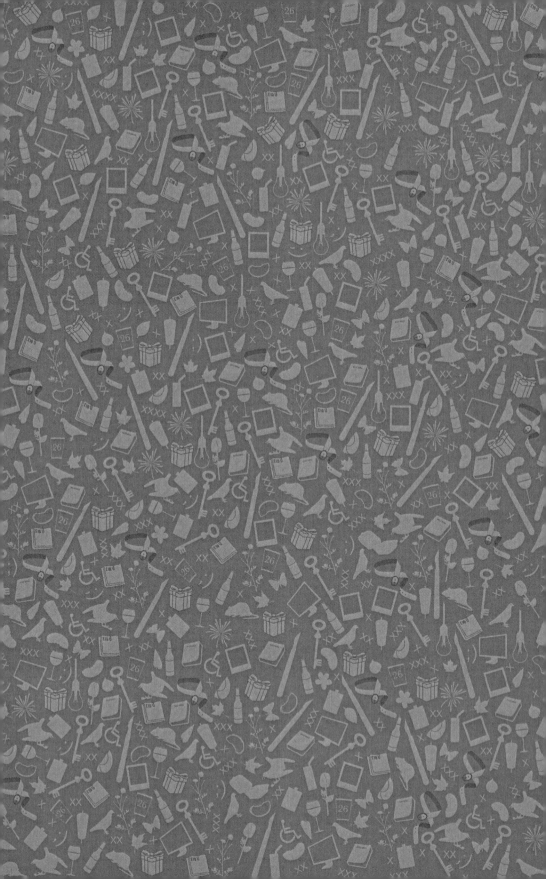

Day 19

The book said to set targets and goals. They had an example by someone who'd been through it and there was a picture of him on the page in full colour. He was sitting at a desk. There was a nameplate in front of him in plated gold. They'd printed his routine that he used to have tacked to his wall: '8.30am – buy a good newspaper.' and '9.00am – check and respond to 'work' emails'.

"I was thinking I could cook tonight. What do you think?" Alex said.

She was fiddling with the hairdryer. Sometimes when she plugged it in it would power up, hum, then shut down. She patted the side of it and something inside rattled.

"Maybe Moroccan Lamb," he said. "Will I get that?"

"Well, pay for it out of the joint account if you do."

"Is anything still to come off?"

"Maybe. Don't spend too much in case."

The hairdryer kicked in but was stuttering. The power going on and off in waves. She'd shake it, the thing would clatter, then right itself for a while.

"Maybe I'll leave the lamb then," Alex said.

The hairdryer cut out.

"You'll have to get that sorted. I could look at it today," he said.

"When?"

"Well, I was going to get a haircut and do the shopping. I've got a couple of other bits and bobs to do but at one point I'll find the time."

"What if you make it worse?"

"Could it get much worse?"

Annie sighed and looked down at it.

"Just use your straighteners to dry your hair," Alex said.

"No. It damages it." She let the hairdryer drop to the bed. "Look, see if I leave you my Boots Card can you go and buy me another one today? There should be enough points, you shouldn't have to add anything to it. Just get a basic one."

"Where's the nearest Boots?"

"Clydebank? There's one at Byres Road."

"I might need to go into town at one point anyway. I could just go there."

"They'll have a bigger selection."

"That's true."

"Thanks," she said.

"And you're sure you don't want me to look at it?"

Annie rested her elbow on his knee.

"Listen to you. A real DIY man. What could you actually even do to fix it?"

He sat up straighter and the covers rode down to his waist.

Annie laughed, "Let's hear it then."

"Well I'd... I'd get a screwdriver and take the panel off."

"What panel's that then?"

"The side one."

"The side one? Is that its official name?"

"I'd remove the board thing, twist a few wires, replace a few fuses, that type of thing. You know, just general electrical maintenance of the," Alex picked up the hairdryer, "Babyliss Prospeed 2100W."

"Oh, you're such a big, tough man," she said.

"It sounds like a fuckin broomstick."

Annie kept up with the on/off process until her hair was somewhere between wet and dry.

"I reckon I'll finish my book today," Alex said.

"How much to go?"

"Fifty pages or so."

"So what's that, about an hour?"

"Something like that."

"I could read it after you then and we could talk about it."

"It's one of the funniest books I've ever read. I don't know if you'll like it though. It's kind of a guy's book."

"A guy's book? Excuse me?"

"No I just mean the things it's about. Like sleeping with lots of women and working in a post office. Plus I don't think you'll like his humour."

"Yet it's one of the best books you've ever read?"

"Well yeah. Here, I'll give you one of his short stories and you can read it on the train. If you like it then you'll probably like the book. It's similar stuff."

"What's the story?"

"I can't remember the name of it. But it's got this guy and he's working in a factory and on his lunch break he goes out to his car and takes drugs with this crazy guy. Then he goes back in and work's better."

Alex laughed at the memory.

"Sounds wonderful," Annie said.

"Later on he goes home to his house and his wife is drunk. He's got these two sons, Rob and Bob... Do you not think that's funny? Rob and Bob?"

"Not really," Annie said.

"Shit, I can't remember what it's called, but I've got it here somewhere. I'll look for it."

"I'm leaving in five minutes," she said.

Alex looked through the pile of papers on his bedside table.

"If I can't find it then I'll email you the story and you can just print it off at work if you want." Papers floated to the floor. "This place is a mess," he said.

"You could try and tidy up today," she said.

"I'll see if I can fit it in."

He saw Annie watching in the reflection of the mirror.

"Just some light reading," he said, dropping sheet after sheet to the floor. It was all stuff he planned to get around to reading. Wikipedia entries on metaphysics, Socialism, Calvinism, Absurdism, Bob Dylan, Woody Allen, juggling.

"Fuck sake," Annie said, straightening down parts of her hair. A steam rose into the air from the strands that were still damp. There was a smell of burning.

"It's not here," Alex said. "The story's not here."

"This stupid fucking hairdryer," she said.

"I'll find it for you for tomorrow. Promise."

They looked at each other in the mirror for a few seconds. They looked at each other and neither of them smiled.

"Your hair's looking good," Alex said.

"It's a mess."

"You still look beautiful."

He climbed across and sat behind her, putting his legs either side of hers.

"Even better when I can see us both," he said.

She looked to the door.

"Like my mingingness makes you even more beautiful you know?" Alex said.

"Maybe you'd look better if you went for a shower," she said.

"I'm going to when you leave."

Annie stood up. She straightened herself in the mirror.

"Can I see your phone quickly?" Alex said.

She was pulling her skirt down lower on her waist.

"It's in my bag. What's wrong with yours?"

"Dead. Can I just see yours?"

Annie sighed. "I don't have time for this."

"Just wanted to know the time."

"It's after eight, I have to go."

"Okay, I suppose I'll see you then."

"Have a nice day. Let me know if you get any good news on the job front."

"I'll email."

"Okay, I'll keep them open."

"Kiss?" Alex said.

"You've not brushed your teeth."

"Annie. Fuck sake," Alex said.

"God, I'm joking, I'm joking. You're so easy."

She walked over. Alex stretched up, put his arms around her and kissed her. She kept her lips together.

"I'll cook a really nice meal," he said.

"Can't wait. I really can't. I love when you cook for me. But don't worry if you can't. If you don't have time."

"I'll have time. I'll just cut down my Playstation time to two hours instead of four."

"The scary thing is I'm not sure if you're kidding."

She walked past him out of the room and he heard the key turning in the lock.

"Bye then," he said.

"Have a good day."

The door closed over and her footsteps echoed back from the stairwell. Alex lay back. He took a pillow from Annie's side and placed it on top of his. There were bits of the papers he'd gone through strewn across the bed. He kicked them to the floor and closed his eyes.

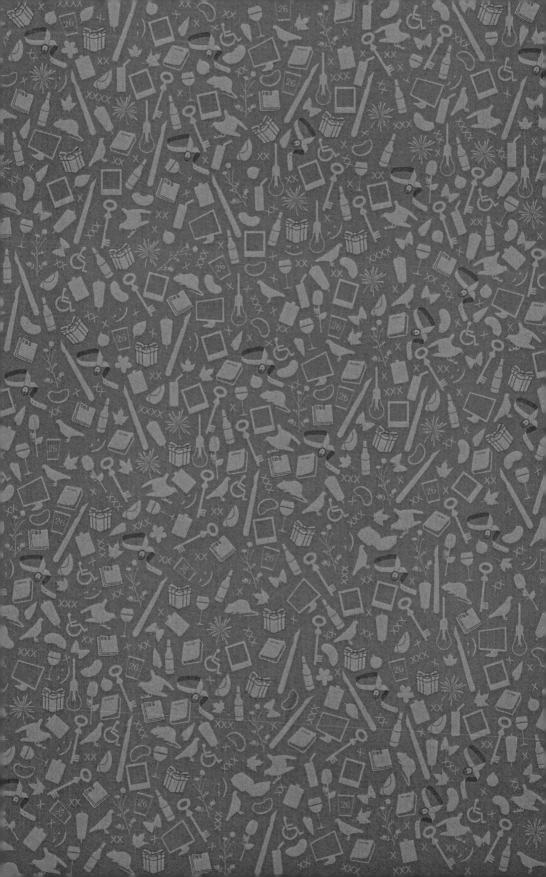

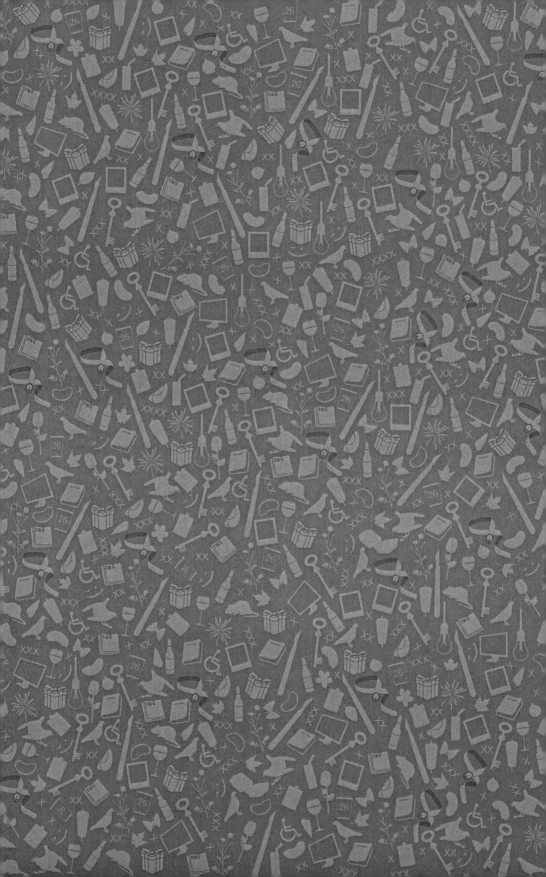

Life Expectancy

Every second Tuesday we met. On the Monday or Sunday I'd put together the diary of my achievements from the previous fortnight. It got so I just made it up, but everyone does that. I used different pens so it didn't look like I'd filled it all in at once. I started getting creative. Saying I'd been looking into working in the UAE. That I'd heard in Aruba a teacher was considered a messiah; further up the status chain than a priest or a poet. I said my top five destinations to work were Aruba, Jamaica, Bermuda, Glasgow and the UAE. That was my order. What could Martin do to help me fulfil my dreams? I said all that during meeting four. Now we were up to meeting six.

"Martin, would I be correct in assuming you want me to die?" I said. "Would that make your life easier? Would that make you a more pleasant person to deal with? Are you bad to your Mother?"

Martin asked me what I'd done to secure employment since our last meeting.

"What if I was to tell you that this week all I did was sit around the house dreaming up ways of driving you out of that chair so I could apply for your job? What if I was to say the only job I want to apply for is Performing Annoyogram? Someone could pay me to handcuff myself to you and I'd swallow the fucking key. You'd have to stay strapped to me – a howling, key-infested me –

until I'd done the deed to relieve myself. Can you sort me out with a position like that Martin?"

Martin pointed to the sign that was tacked to the pin board behind his desk –
"We will not tolerate physical or verbal abuse of our staff."

The sign was positioned at an angle. Like it had been barged by a shoulder.

"What is that underneath the writing?" I said.

Martin didn't even turn. He kept his eyes on mine.

"It's Braille," he says. "You don't recognise Braille Mr McKellar?"

Martin explained to me that my requirements for procuring employment were unrealistic. That if I didn't accept a suitable position soon then we had a serious fiscal problem.

"I'm not even wanting benefits," I said. "I only take the benefits so I can get meetings with you."

"I'll recommend they stop then," Martin said.

I shrugged. I smiled.

Martin sighed and typed something up.

"You really want me dead," I said. "My God, I see it now. You actually fantasise about me being in the ground. Christ Martin, you really are a piece of work. There's evil in you, man."

"Look!"

He slapped his hands down on the desk. A few people turned. He loosened his collar and continued more calmly. "If you were dead then I'd be out of a job. If you were dead then I'd be you. Trust me, for that reason alone I don't want you dead."

I sat back in my chair. I was nodding and stroking my stubble. I thought about what Martin said for a while. I pointed at him when I understood.

"They want you dead too Martin. They want me dead first. But after I'm gone they want you dead. It's simple economics. Cut the funding of the NHS, cut the funding to schools. Over time, life expectancy will drop. They want you to live until the ripe old age of sixty-five and a day. That's the stuff these guys dream of. They dream of your deterioration at an alarming rate. Tell you Martin, the average life expectancy of a retired teacher is eighteen months. That'd have been me. Jesus, if that's the case I'll be dead by thirty. What is it for a person in your position? Do you know? What is your position? Would it be disrespectful of me to call you a lackey?"

"Senior Employment Advisor," he said.

"Well Christ! Senior? You should have said. That's a title they'll try and take away from you. Soon you'll be just an employment advisor. Then they'll decide a man of your skill should be advising on all manner of matters – teenage pregnancy, bereavement, which supermarket best suits a person's needs, and then you'll be known only as advisor. Martin the advisor. What do you think about that?"

"I'm going to advise you no longer qualify for Job Seekers Allowance," Martin told me.

"You're a cold man, Martin."

"Unless there's anything else?" he said.

"What about a kiss?"

"Well we'll be seeing you then Mr McKellar. It's been a pleasure."

I stood up.

"Don't you worry about me Martin. Soon I'll be in Aruba, Jamaica, ooh I wanna take ya... You know that song, Martin?"

Martin was typing and didn't look up. The security guard walked beside me as I walked backwards through the automatic doors.

"The Beach Boys, Martin," I called.

The automatic doors shut and the security guard stood in front of them, between me and the inside of the building. The doors opened and closed a few times. Him standing there with his arms folded.

"How did you get that job, big man?" I said.

The security guard didn't answer.

I zipped up my jacket and pulled the hood over my head. The lights from Gennaro's chippy were up ahead. I blew into my hands. My breath turned smoky in the air. I began to walk. Then I started to run. As fast as I could. A car swerved beside me. When I looked back, the woman from Gennaro's had her head out the door and was staring. The driver of the car was pointing after me. I made it on to Great Western Road and ran towards the west. I ran down the centre of the road, following the white lines. I slapped the sides of cars and buses when I passed them. I laughed out loud. A taxi driver put his hand out his window and called me a wank. The air was cloudy with exhaust fumes. The horizon didn't look too far. If I could keep going I'd reach Loch Lomond. If I could keep going I'd reach the sea.

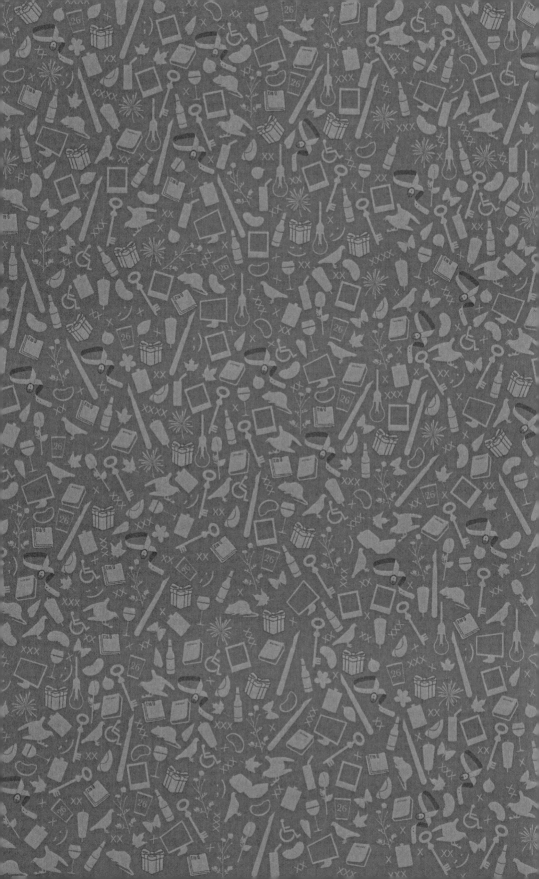

Swimming with Sharks and Bungee Jumping

The shark swim was more expensive, but I couldn't see any way Gordon could have done that without me knowing. They had other gifts too like helicopter rides, Ferrari racing and aerobatic stunt flying, but those lacked the thrill. It had to be the sharks or the jump.

The problem with traditional Christmas shopping is the people. Everywhere you go there's a face. And the truth is, I've known a lot of men. If we were on the street or in the shopping centre there's always the feeling that I'll be recognised. I understand why people turn out crazy.

Now let's get one thing straight: I'm not scared of him. Gordon's smarter than me when it comes to the details. He remembers what I forget. Even when I'm certain, when he remembers differently, chances are I'm wrong. I'm sure that our first year together I bought us an artificial tree but he says he got us a real one. Norwegian pine, he says. Every year since he's been the one that buys the tree. Like he has to rub it in.

It was Colin, a colleague in work, who came up with the adventure day. He told me the website and I checked. They send it next day delivery in a gift wrapped box. All the recipient has to do is say what date they want their experience to happen and complete a form online.

I remember it was the eighth of December we went shopping because it's the date John Lennon died. I'd picked out every gift I was giving by then. All that was left was to decide between the two options for Gordon. He hadn't even begun. He'll see something in a shop, check a hundred others then go back and buy the thing he saw in the first place. When I came out of the shower I put on Woman. He was still asleep so I turned it up loud and sang in his ear.

"Ooooh, well, well."

He stirred and pulled the covers over his head.

"Doo do do doo do."

"That time of year already?"

"Another year without him."

"Turn it down a bit can you."

I walked over to the stereo and lowered the volume.

"If we get in early we can beat the crowds."

"Five minutes and I'll get up."

His voice was muffled beneath the blankets so I turned the song quieter.

"I'll be ready for nine so as long as you're ready for nine."

"Turn it down a bit more," he said.

"That?"

"Bit more."

It was so low you had to lean towards the speaker.

"Bit more."

I turned until the dial jarred.

"Ahh, that's better. Let's just keep it like that shall we?"

"You've four minutes then up. Hope you're glad."

"Very."

He turned to face the other way.

Yoko Ono says that December eighth should be a day of forgiveness. That on this day we should remember John and everyone else who has died. That we should remember those who are in situations in which they may be in danger of death. Forgive those situations and those people. But she can't forgive Mark Chapman. No matter what she tries.

Even at ten in the morning the shops were packed. Debenhams were doing a double discount day and there were queues leading from the clothes' rails to the counters. Gordon was stroking a dressy white shirt.

"Your Dad will like it," I said. "If you change your mind we can bring it back but you might as well get it now because if you don't somebody else will."

"Do you really think it's his style though?"

"Definitely."

"But is it not quite similar to the shirt we got him for his birthday? I think it's too similar."

"That shirt was blue."

"I know but it's more the style I'm thinking about."

"Get it and then we'll bring it back if need be."

He held it up and examined it.

"I don't know. It's maybe not something he'd wear."

"Just get it and then we can return it."

He looked it over once more and held it against his chest.

"It's not jumping out at me. I'll wait until I see something jumping out at me."

He hung the shirt back on the rail.

Now the thing about being a nurse is you learn patience. You learn to let it ease in then let it out. On the other hand you meet so many people. If someone looks at me in public I wonder if they are patients or staff. I've heard of couples who have five that don't count lists. Sex without concequences. It's fantasy. But to think of him inside of someone else makes me sick.

I make a thousand acquaintances. That's what Gordon doesn't get: they're not my friends, not my lovers, they're acquaintances. They know my name, they know my face, they know what I want them to know. But they don't know me. I don't have it so easy. In Gordon's office there's only the four men.

At lunchtime he suggested Geronimo's. I wasn't hungry so ordered soup. Our waitress's name was Debbie and Gordon smirked while he asked her how Geronimo was.

"Em, I'll ask the manager," she said.

"Do you think Geronimo's a real name?" he asked me.

"Why do you bother? She's just a girl."

"I wonder what the manager will say."

He stretched up in his seat and looked over the back of our booth. It'd be less embarrassing being married to a taller man.

The manager came over when we were halfway through our meal.

"Is everything okay with your food?"

I smiled. Gordon said the meat was a little over cooked but, apart from that, everything was hitting the spot.

"I will change that for you."

"Nah it's fine. Just so you're aware of the problem."

"Thank you sir. Geronimo is not here anymore sir."

"Oh," Gordon put down his knife and fork, "so there was a Geronimo?"

"He sold the place to us."

"Is he alive?"

"As far as I know sir."

"Well at least that's something eh?"

"Yes sir."

Gordon laughed.

"Thank you sir."

"Thanks."

The manager went away.

"Happy now?" I said.

"Don't get lippy. I thought it was a brand name."

We shopped until darkness. The cold came down and I bought myself a woolly hat. There was a German market on and we bought bratwursts for dinner. Gordon asked for chillies but they didn't do them. He shrugged and ate the sausage in three bites.

On the Sunday he read the papers and I looked at gifts online. Sharks or Bungee? I looked over at Gordon. On Sundays, when he washes his hair and puts no products in, it goes fluffy and spikes in the air.

"I think I'll go and get us a tree today," he said.

"We could do it next week."

"We could... Or I could get it today."

"When would we put it up?"

"Today."

We looked at each other.

"You get the decorations from the loft whilst I'm getting the tree," he said. "Get in the Christmas spirit for God sake."

I looked for more information online when he was out. The Youtube videos of bungee jumping showed grown men squealing. There weren't many of shark swims. I found a man from Cheshire saying he'd got up close with sharks at a sealife centre. He said it was no more dangerous than swimming with a goldfish. But there was another man, Stuart from Edinburgh, who'd done it at North Queensferry, where Gordon would be doing it. He described it by saying, "I'm forty three, twice married with four kids. Never in all my life have I done anything as crazy as the shark dive. You get so close you can see guts in their teeth. I thought I was going to die." I booked it there and then.

It'd be easy to say that Gordon hitting me is unjustified. Maybe it is. But when I told him I'd slept with those other men I couldn't stop the words sprouting from my mouth. I kept telling him more and more about it. The details a nurse gets to know. You know what's normal about the human body and what isn't. I had a warm feeling when I was telling him. I gave him details about my other lovers that no man would ever want to know. The hard thing would have been to have held on to the truth. There's an honour in a lie that never leaves you.

I told him about my year on and off with Jonathan, the one drunken night with Eddie and my on the job sessions with Dr Ray. We sat in silence for a long time after I told him. He let me hold his hand.

He tried to give me a baby for over two years after that. I suppose for some people that's just how it goes. After that we stopped trying and every now and again he hits me. I'm not complaining, some lives just work out that way.

Mark Chapman is eligible for parole every two years but so far it has always been denied. Yoko Ono says we should forgive people who wrong us but she can't forgive Mark Chapman. He says it was Holden Caulfield that told him to kill John. He was insane the day he got his gun and fired those bullets. He couldn't do anything right his whole life except murder. He thought John knew where the ducks went in winter. He shot him because he loved him.

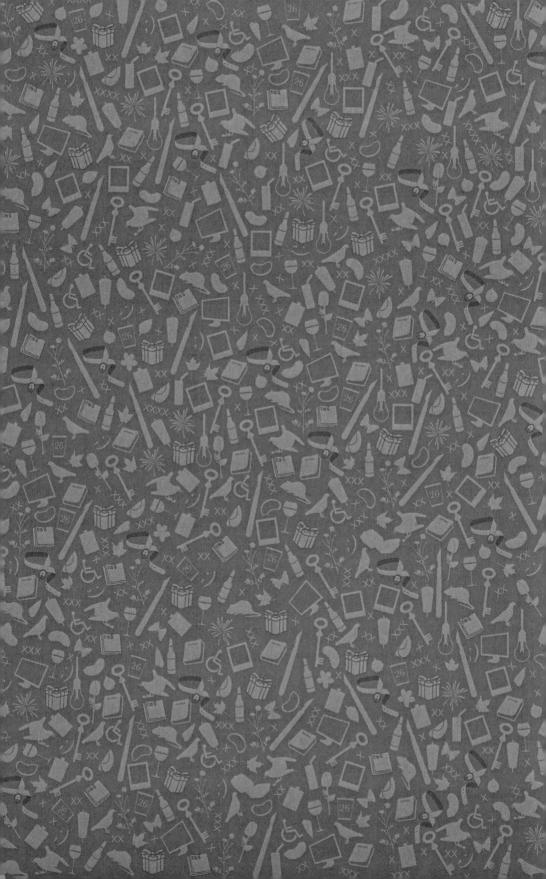

Thunder

"Uncle Johnny!" the kid squealed.

John thought that normally kids with missing teeth looked cute. The gaps at the front of their mouths waiting for the adult teeth to fill them. Not this one though. He looked like he'd finished second in a fight.

"That ain't your Uncle, kiddo. John is your brother."

Bill came over smiling. He was slim and tanned. He shook hands with John, then pulled him in for a hug.

"How was the flight?" he asked.

"Well, the food was spectacular," John said.

"Yeah, I bet. But at least you've made it to the good old US of A now," Bill said.

He began to laugh and put his arm around John's shoulder.

"You know John, I'd say you've put on a bit of timber since last year. What do you think?"

Ella was standing by the exit. The kid was by her side now, sucking on a chocolate bar. As Bill and John approached, Ella let out a cry and ran forwards for a hug.

"I'm just saying to the boy Ella, he's looking bigger this year, don't you think?"

Ella stepped back and looked John up and down. She stroked his arm as she spoke.

"John," she said. "You're looking really great John. All the better for it. You were too skinny before. You've a healthy look about you. A glow. You gotta come visit more often. You ain't even seen the new place yet."

She leant back in and kissed his cheek.

"That's plenty, that's plenty," his Dad said. Then he began to laugh.

Ella hit Bill's arm. "Ha. Ha. Very funny," she said. She turned to John. "He thinks I want to trade him in for a younger model, that's his problem."

Ella and Bill began to paw at each other. The kid got involved too, pulling at John's arm and holding up his haunches for a fight. He took John's hand and pressed it hard on his forehead.

"You got me Uncle John, you got me? Make sure you hold me."

The kid started to push with all his weight against John's palm, butting it with his head. John's footing faltered on the linoleum and he had to step back for balance.

"See how strong I am?" the kid said.

Ella and Bill had stopped playing and were looking at the two sons.

"He's gonna be six foot six and built like a bull," Bill said, nodding towards the kid. "He's got weights at home, can you believe that? Bought them himself. Everyday he's up there doing all sorts of exercises. Moves I don't even know about."

The kid was still pushing his head against John's palm. His eyes were squeezed closed and his face was bright pink.

"That's enough now Joseph," Ella said.

The kid carried on.

Ella looked at John. "Just you take your hand away darling. He'll stop if you stop pushing back."

"You think?" John said.

"Oh yeah, he does this all the time."

"If I take my hand away he's gonna keep going. His head will go through that wall."

"Joseph!" Bill shouted. "Heel boy, heel!"

The kid stopped pressing and stood to attention. He saluted.

"Sir, yes sir!"

"Good boy. Now carry your brother's suitcase to the car. Off you go, that's it."

The kid grabbed the bag and heaved it with both hands. Every so often he'd stop, stretch his fingers then hold the handles. He tensed so much that tendons stuck out his neck like roots. Then he'd lift again. The others stood back and watched.

"I guess I'll be the one to help him then," Ella said.

When she'd gone, Bill put his arm back around John and they followed Ella and the kid towards the car park.

"So how's life? Good?" he asked.

"Yeah, life's good."

"How's your Mother?"

"Just the same. Working away. Getting on with it."

"Ella's expecting," Bill said. "Is she showing?"

John stopped walking and watched Ella and the kid carrying his bag.

"Really? I didn't know. I didn't really look."

"Twelve weeks," Bill said. "Don't mention it though, let her tell you herself if she wants to."

Ella had a hand on the bag while the kid used two. They were moving at a good pace now and the men were far enough behind that they wouldn't be heard.

"Well aren't you going to congratulate your old Dad?"

"Of course, aye. Well done. Good job. Did you plan it?"

"Are you serious? I want to have a whole bunch of them. A whole football team's worth running around after me. You're the captain though, and Joseph can be vice. You know how it is. You try for years then they all come along at once, right?"

They walked for a while towards the car park. Ella and the kid had disappeared in a lift and John stopped to wait for the next one. His Dad tutted and led them to the stairs.

"Elevators," he said, "they'll be the death of you. Climbing stairs is the best form of exercise out there. You climb the stairs, you eat your vitamins and you live until you're a hundred years old. I've seen it with my own eyes. Take Ella's Dad. He's in his eighties. He did an Ironman last year. That's me. That's exactly how I'm gonna be."

John began to laugh.

"Dad, I'm just thinking. When Joseph turns ten you'll be sixty, right?"

Bill thought for a few seconds.

"I guess so," he said.

"So when this new baby is born, when it turns ten, you'll be what, pushing seventy-one? That's fucking mental."

Bill stopped walking and turned to his son. He was quiet for a long time. For a while it looked as if he might shout something or turn away in disgust. But that didn't happen. Bill began to laugh.

"There's life in me yet," he said. "If Ella's pipes are still working I'll be firing them out when I'm seventy-five, eighty, a hundred."

He laughed loudly. When John caught up, Bill put his arm back around his shoulder.

"It really is great to see you. The thing I miss most about home? It's the banter. Good old Scottish banter. We should go out for a drink later. I know a little place that sells Tennent's."

In the car on the way back the kid asked to ride up front with his Dad, and Ella had climbed into the back before he got an answer. Not long into the journey the kid slouched down in his chair and began making sounds like a laser gun.

"What's he doing now Bill?" Ella said.

"It's his game," Bill said. "See that crack on the windshield? That little hairline? He thinks it's a rocket ship. He steers us over trees and buildings."

Bill ruffled the kid's hair and drove on. He spoke quietly to the kid while John and Ella had a conversation in the back. Ella sat with her hands covering her stomach.

"Now tell me John," she said. "Because you see, I get a feeling for these things. Is there someone special in your life? I see a glow about you, I really do. If you were a stranger and I had to guess, I'd say you were in love."

John saw his Dad's eyes flash in the rear view mirror. He popped his eyebrows up and down then went back to messing with the kid.

John felt himself beginning to blush. Not that being in love was such a bad thing. More that it was, well, it was something he'd never speak to his own Mother about. He wondered if Ella saw herself as his Mother. Even in some surrogate type way. Even during the years he'd shouted and screamed at her, called her every swear word he knew. It took a long time for him to accept what had happened. Ella was so different from his Mum. A different type of person altogether. After a few years of transatlantic crossings, John told his Mum there was nothing selfish or cruel about his Dad after all. And she should know that too.

"I'm right ain't I?" Ella began to dig him in the ribs. "Say it, say I'm right." She called through to the front of the car. There was a lilt in her voice. "Oh Bill, guess what? Johnny's in love."

His Dad looked in the mirror again and winked. He gave a thumbs up and went back to looking at the road. The kid took off his seatbelt and turned right around in his chair.

"Ooooh, who is she Uncle John? What's her name? Is she hot?"

Ella kept digging John's ribs. "Well tell us will you."

"Okay, okay. Her name's Arabella. Belle. We only met this year but it..."

The kid began to laugh.

"John and Arab Ella, sitin in a tree. K-I-S-S-I-N-G."

Ella spoke in between laughter. She blushed and held her hand up in apology. "Joseph, sit back down."

"You didn't mention her on the phone," his Dad called back.

"You didn't ask," John replied.

Ella leant across John and pushed the kid's shoulder. "Bill make him sit down," she said.

Bill stretched his palm around the seat and Ella took hold of it.

"Joseph! Heel boy, heel!"

The kid twisted round, sat tall and straight, faced the windscreen and saluted.

"Sir, yes sir!" he said.

"It is fifteen hundred hours private, am I right?" Bill said.

The kid turned his wrist and raised it in front of his eyes.

"Not exactly sir. It is 1503, sir!"

"Damn it private, we are behind! Now put on your safety belt and let's get to work."

The kid strapped up and kept his back solid against the seat.

"Sir, permission to turn to Uncle John sir?"

"Okay private. But keep that safety belt tight."

"Sir yes sir!" The kid twisted around to face John. "What kind of name is Arab Ella?" he said. "Is she an I-raqi or something?"

John saw his Dad's eyes flash in the mirror and Ella buried her head in the gap between John's shoulder and neck. Then everyone, the whole car load except John, began to laugh.

In their new home John had a room to himself. In the old, two-bedroom apartment he had a room but when the kid was born it became his room and John would sleep in the attic whenever he visited. He liked the attic. It stretched the entire length of the apartment and the heat rose from the rooms below. He would lie in bed and listen to what was happening downstairs. He used to close his eyes and pretend he was a child again. He saw himself as a boy in a film who had been so cheeky he'd been sent there. John would joke to himself that in the morning they'd have disappeared and he'd have the whole place to himself. He'd wear their clothes and watch their TVs.

Ella, or at least he guessed it was Ella, had tried to dot some home comforts about to make the new room his. There was a framed picture from a few years back of the four of them on a fishing trip with the kid holding up a fish, his finger in its gullet and sticking out through the mouth. There was a flag that was half a saltire and half the stars and stripes draped along the wall above the headboard.

There was a knock on the door.

"Hey, Uncle John," the kid said, "do you like wrestling?"

The kid walked in with his top off. He had bandages wrapped around his wrists and was wearing long shorts that read THUNDER along the belt.

"I take it you do," John said.

"Yeah, wrestling is okay but I prefer boxing now. What do you like?"

"I used to like wrestling. When I was a kid."

"When I get to Junior High I'm going to join the wrestling team. They don't let you box. My Dad says that in Scotland everyone likes boxing."

"Aye, maybe on a Friday night."

The kid walked over to the mirror and started throwing punches at his reflection.

"I'm the biggest boy in my class," he said. "Some people think I'm twelve."

He stood with his hands on his hips and faced John.

"What do you think?"

"You could pass for twelve I'd say, yeah."

The kid smiled and started throwing uppercuts really quickly.

"Mohammed Ali, Mike Tyson, me. Me, me, me, me, me!" he said.

When he finished he was red again and his face was wet around the lips. John had inherited that ruddy complexion too.

"Let's have an arm wrestle," the kid said.

He walked over to John and cleared a space on the vanity table. He wasn't careful. He knocked the deodorant over and swept a small basket of pot pourri onto the floor. He didn't seem to notice he was doing it. The kid was focussed. The kid was pumped.

"Careful wee man," John said, "seven years bad luck if you smash a mirror you know."

"The way I see it, you make your own luck," the kid said. Then he picked up the mirror and dropped it on the bed. It bounced a few times before settling on the duvet.

"You ready?" he said. He placed his elbow on the wood and, with his red face still shining around the mouth, looked up at John.

John remembered being young and doing the same thing. His Dad would roll up his sleeve and beat his chest like a gorilla. "Oh I'm gonna get you," he'd say. "I'm gonna get you this time." John would laugh at his Dad or make threats. His Dad would struggle during the arm wrestle, go red. He'd let John take him to the brink of defeat. He'd wait until his hand almost touched the deck and then he'd begin the comeback. Make groaning noises, scream, "I have the power!" and pull it back to equal. After that it was touch and go. Sometimes he'd let John win, other times he'd teach him a lesson.

The kid began a running commentary.

"In the blue corner we have Joseph 'Thunder' Jones versus John 'The Stinker'..."

"Jones," John said.

"John 'The Stinker' Jones. Ding, ding, ding. Round one."

John walked over and stood opposite the boy.

"Don't you be cheating," the kid said. "Other hand behind your back and no holding on."

John did as he was told. They gripped hands and the kid stared into John's eyes.

"I'll count down from three," he said. "When I say go we start. Up until then, no pressure. That's the rules."

John smiled and waggled his eyebrows up and down at the kid.

"Something funny stinker?" the kid said.

"Nah man, I'm just waiting on you."

"So it's like that is it? Okay. Okay. Let's do this then. We got a tough guy here, oh yeah."

The kid turned his neck from side to side until it cracked. When it did he licked his lips then began the countdown.

"Three, two..."

"Wait," John said. "Don't we need an independent adjudicator or something?"

The kid looked confused.

"I mean shouldn't we get Dad and your Mum?"

The kid stopped to think for a while then nodded. "Well if you're that scared..." He let out a wail. "Mum... Dad... Come in here."

There was a heavy tread in the hallway, then Bill strode in looking worried. Ella wasn't far behind. When they saw Joseph and the way he was dressed they stopped. Bill turned to Ella and she shook her head.

"There's the little man," Bill said. "There's the champ."

"Mum, Dad," the kid said, "John wants you to be here when I beat him down."

The kid kept his eyes on John as he spoke. Their hands were still together. His chest heaved in and out.

John looked to his Dad and Ella then shrugged. His Dad gave him a wink.

"Okay champ," Bill said. "I'd pay good money to see this."

Bill and Ella sat on the bed. When Ella noticed the mess Joseph had made on the floor she knelt down and started picking up the pieces of pot pourri.

"Leave that," Bill said. "Get up here and watch the show."

Ella shook her head. "If somebody stands on this it'll stain."

"A woman's work," Bill said. "Okay boys are we getting started here?"

The kid twisted his neck from side to side again until it cracked.

"Don't do that baby," Ella called up. "You'll damage your spine."

Bill looked at both his sons then rolled his eyes. He stood up and cupped his hands over theirs. He cleared his throat.

"I got a feeling this is gonna be a close one," he said. "There's a lot of strength in both these arms. Now, I'll count backwards from three. When I say go, you boys can fight it out. Don't move an inch until I say go."

"You're goin down sucka!" the kid yelled.

"Bill, tell him not to speak like that to John," Ella called up.

Bill shook his head.

"Sure thing honey."

He leant in close to his sons. He faced Joseph, and John couldn't see his face. He whispered something in the kid's ear and the kid's laughter burst out through his nose. When Bill turned around to face John he winked. "I think this is going to be a close contest," he said, "a really close contest." He winked again.

"Okay. Three, two, one, go!"

The pressure kicked in. There was some real power in the kid's arm. John felt like he was holding tight against someone much older. He looked to Bill who was nodding and smiling. Even Ella had knelt up high to watch. The kid was really going for it. Taking little sharp breaths as he pushed. John felt his hand moving towards the wood. He tensed his muscles and managed to hold his hand still a few inches off the table top.

"Feel the burn sucka!" the kid said.

But John could feel the pressure lessen a little as the kid started to run out of steam. There was no denying Joseph was strong. In a few years time he'd probably be a real match for any adult. John began to put his own strength into the bout. He took the kid's arm back up to the midway point. John started to groan. "I didn't know you'd be so strong," he told the kid. The kid's face was bright pink. There was a sweat on his forehead and his gapped rows of teeth were pressed hard together. John put some pressure on, taking the kid's hand down towards the deck. But then he let the kid back to centre. "I don't know how much longer I can go on," John said. They stayed at gridlock for a while. John could see his Dad's eyes on him. In the background Ella's head stretched up and she kept turning every so often to look at Bill.

The kid strained to speak. "I'm too strong for you," he said. "Give it up, just give it up."

John put strain in his own voice. "Never," he said. "Never will I admit defeat."

And then, before he knew it, John had slammed the kid's hand down on the wood. He stood up and held his hands high above his head. Bill and Ella were silent. But it was only a moment. A split second where he knew what they were thinking.

"Fuck, shit, motherfucker," the kid shouted.

"Joseph!" Ella said. "Bill, tell him not to speak like that. Tell him."

The kid pounded the table top with his fist. His face was bright red. Ella stood up to put her arms around him and he jammed his elbows into the side of her body then ran, still shouting, out of the room. But it was Ella's face. How all the colour just left it. Her knees seemed to buckle as Bill stepped over and grabbed her forearms.

"Tell me what's wrong," he said.

Ella cupped her hands just below her stomach.

"I feel sick," she said. "I feel sick."

Bill looked up at John. He didn't speak. The only sounds John heard were the kid stomping around upstairs. The floor creaking as he jumped and shouted. Then Ella. The way she kept repeating the same words as Bill led her out the room.

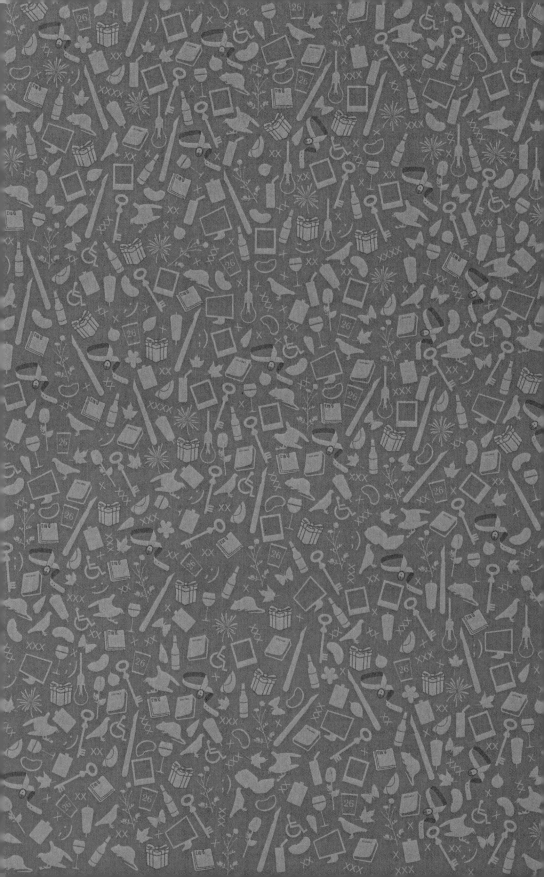

The Marijuana Room

Susie, whose flat we are viewing, calls it a second bedroom. "Although it's wee Robbie's room now," she says, "before that we used it as an office-cum, I don't know, games room I suppose. Bob's quite into retro gaming so he had a few TVs and some old games systems in here." She leans her head out the doorway and calls through to the living room. "How many tellies was it you had in here Bob?"

"Seven," he shouts back.

Susie sweeps her arm across the room. "Hence the plug sockets."

Annie laughs.

"So yeah, it's a decent size. The estate agents have labelled it as a one bedroom but we think it's really a two bedroom." She puts her hand on the cot.

The wee boy is sitting on the floor in the far corner of the room. He is sucking the back of his hand. Susie walks over and lifts him up. She carries him over to us. "Say hello Robbie." The wee boy puts his hand back in his mouth and sucks. "He's just turned eighteen months," Susie says.

Annie strokes his cheek with her finger. "He's gorgeous," she says.

Susie and Robbie show us round the rest of the flat: the decent-sized kitchen, fully equipped with dishwasher; the long, galley style bathroom, fully equipped with Robbie's potty; the living room with bay window and Bob on the couch.

"He's got a big meeting at work tomorrow," Susie whispers, "he's not being rude."
She leads us to the bedroom and leaves us by ourselves. She closes the door.
Robbie's gargling disappears from earshot.

"So what do you think?"

"I really like it," I say. "I mean I really, really like it."

"Me too."

"How long has this one been on?" I ask.

"Only two days. When I called the estate agent she said there's no way it won't
go within a week."

We look at each other.

"I love the high ceilings," Annie says.

I walk to her and lean in. I whisper in her ear. "There's no way they've priced
this right." "They've priced it as a one bedroom but that room definitely makes it
a two."

She pulls away and looks at me.

"So what should we do?"

"I love it," she says, "I love it."

I take her hand and walk out the room. Susie is rocking Robbie and they
are standing over Bob. He seems to be complaining about the work he is doing.
He wipes his eyes with the base of his palms.

Susie looks over. "So is all okay? Anything else you want to know or anything?"

"Yeah, I think so," I say. "It's a really nice flat. How many people have you
had up?"

Susie thinks for a second. "Well it was advertised first on Monday. We had one
couple up on Monday night, they had a wee boy as well, and then you two and later
on tonight we've got another viewer. After that it's, I don't know, another four or five
this week, something like that. The estate agent keeps calling, asking if people can
come up, but you know what it's like, and I don't like people coming when Bob's
not here."

Annie is nodding her head and grinning.

"Yeah, absolutely," I say.

The kid, little Robbie, begins to cry. Susie shoogles him but he doesn't stop.
She bends over and holds him out for Bob. "Can you take him to the potty," she says.

Bob piles the papers from his lap to the coffee table. He lifts the wee man under
the arms then stands up. "Excuse me folks," he says, "We've got a code brown here."

"Bob!" Susie says.

Bob calls back over his shoulder. "Honesty is the best policy dear."

Susie laughs and speaks to Annie. "Sorry about that, he's a big kid sometimes."

Annie points her thumb at me. "He's the same."

The two women laugh. I look down. Annie is moving from foot to foot.

We pull in to get petrol. I put a fiver in the tank. As a treat I buy a can of Relentless for us to share. When you drink that stuff on an empty stomach the caffeine gives you a feeling like alcohol.

Little sips then a pass. That's how we do it.

"What did you think when you saw that second room?" she says.

"I thought it was amazing. The whole place. I thought the bedroom was perfect. I can see us there." I lower my voice and say, "I was going to try and have a cheeky moment there and then."

Annie says, "I'm not going to pretend the thought didn't cross my mind, that's all I'm saying."

"Can you imagine it? Doing it in there I mean? In a new place like that?"

She nods and smiles so I grab her thigh just above the knee where it tickles. "I thought you were Little Miss Innocent as well?"

She screams until I loosen my grip.

"I am Little Miss Innocent," she says.

Annie leans over the handbrake and kisses my cheek. "I really love that flat, Alex."

"I like it too," I say. "Let's make a bid on it tonight."

She laughs.

I pull away so she can look at me and know I mean it.

"When they call us tomorrow to ask how we got on I'll say we want another viewing."

"Do we need to get another viewing? Can we not just bid?"

"No, we need to get another viewing. We can take my Mum up with us and take your Dad and get their opinion. And your Dad can check out all the electrical stuff and things."

"Make it for tomorrow night then, what do you think?" I say.

"Yeah, if they can fit us in. You heard what she said, they seem quite busy."

"I think they liked us but. And they could see how keen we are so they should let us back up."

Annie shakes the gearstick. "I really love that extra room as well. We could make it into anything we want. We could have a study and I could paint or we could start a business, anything. We can do whatever we want."

"Yeah, or we could grow hash plants."

She stares at me.

"There's enough plugs for the lights at least," I say.

"Alex, you're not using my beautiful study to grow hash in."

"Could be a nice little earner, that's all I'm saying. Could mean neither of us have to work and we could spend more time together in our amazing flat."

"Well, I suppose that part sounds quite appealing."

"It's settled then," I say. "Spare room is the marijuana room." I list ideas on my fingers. "Some Bob Marley music in the background, put your hair into dreadlocks, put my hair into dreadlocks, keep it always at forty degrees…"

"You're taking this too far now," Annie says.

"Maybe. It's a brilliant room though. Definitely big enough for a double bed."

"I think we'd have to just put a single in it. Or maybe get a sofa bed that pulls out. If we had a double in it we'd not be able to fit anything else."

"I suppose," I say.

Annie holds on to the Relentless and the light from the forecourt is so bright I can see drops of condensation sliding down the can. She is tapping her fingers on the aluminium along to the music on the radio.

"Do you ever get scared though?" I say.

"About what?"

"About getting a flat."

"Do you?"

I take the Relentless from her and have a sip. "I don't think so. I mean I don't, but like, it's a big deal. It'll mean that's it. For the next twenty five years that's it."

"That's what people do."

"I know, but just sometimes I think, what if I want to quit my job and just run away to South America or Japan or something?"

"Is that what you want to do?"

"I don't know what I want to do."

"On your own?"

"No. I don't mean that. I just mean, I don't know. I get scared that the flat will limit us. It's like having a kid."

She takes the Relentless and tips it high, draining the can. We are quiet for a while. I don't turn the engine on. I turn the radio down, then off. I hear gargling from Annie's insides.

"I just really hate my job. I think that's the problem."

"I hate mine as well," she says. "But what's the alternative?"

A car draws into the garage and a man gets out, pulling at the pump behind me. I watch him struggle in my rear view mirror.

"Maybe there's something quite noble about taking from the state if you're doing it for the right reasons. Like if you think about it philosophically. Not just because you can't be fucked getting a job, but 'cause you're saying fuck you to all the nonsense. Fuck you to being a commodity. We never asked to be born into this.

I mean who decided that for forty years of your life you've to wake up miserable every day, work in a job you hate, go away from, from you – the person I love – to be with people I don't care about? Who decided that stuff?"

She sits back.

"People choose to do it because it means they can do things like go on nice holidays, like go out to pubs and nightclubs. Like buy nice flats," she says.

"Sometimes I just think it doesn't have to be this way. All I want is to hang out with you."

"Aww, that's sweet Alex... But you're talking shit."

"I'm not, I'm being serious. That's all I want to do. That's the only time I'm happy and..."

Annie interrupts me. "So going to Paris at Christmas wasn't nice? Couldn't have done that with no money. Meeting your friends every Tuesday? How much do you spend those nights? Fifty pounds? Sixty is it?"

"I don't spend that much. Anyway, you're missing my point. My point is that there must be a better way than the way we're doing it at the moment."

Annie sighs. "I don't know why you always have to do this."

"Do what?" I say, lifting my hands high off the steering wheel.

Annie shakes her head then stares out the passenger window.

I start the car up. "Put on your seatbelt," I say.

"I loved that flat and now it's tainted."

"It's not tainted. I love the flat, I'm just saying..."

"It is tainted."

The second bedroom is a good size. Definitely big enough for a bed. Definitely big enough for a kid's bedroom. Just it's internal so there's no window. But we would maybe be able to paint a mural on the walls if it ever came to it, like a nature scene, sheep grazing in a field or something; something a kid might choose. Dinosaurs on horseback. I guess that's why they are moving out, for their own son. Susie and Bob and wee Robbie. Susie at home looking after him and Bob rubbing his tired eyes with his palms. They'll be moving to some three bedroom semi in Bearsden or something. Somewhere with a garden and nice neighbours and good schools. They are ahead of us. Robbie will grow up and one day he'll go a drive with his girlfriend and show her the first place he ever lived. Maybe me and Annie will have lived there for a while. Maybe we'll have had kids there.

That's if we get the flat. All we've done is view it for twenty minutes and now here we are. In silence. It's nothing big. Not the type of thing that should warrant a night on the couch, but it is an argument. We will sleep apart. And tomorrow we will go away from each other to work.

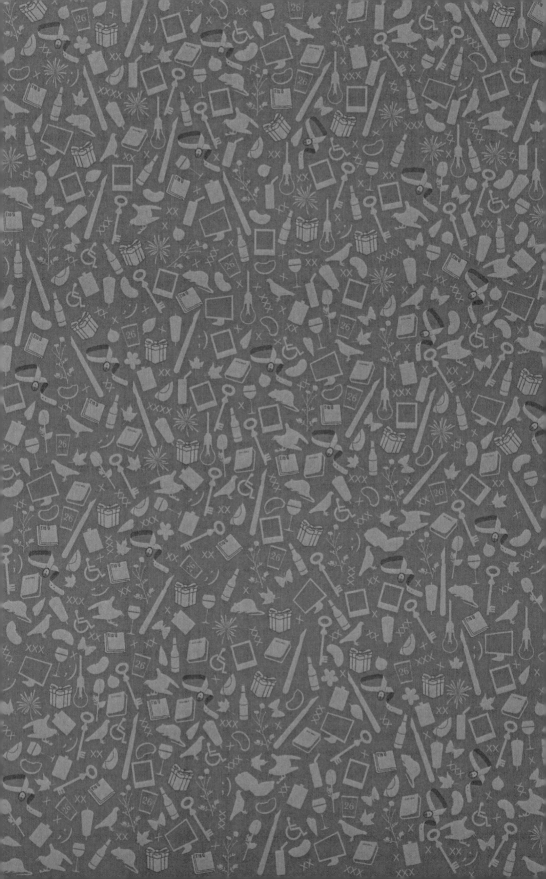

Everyone Will be Orphans

Instead of sheets on the bed, dirty tablecloths. We sat down on the edge.
Me first, bouncing to check the springs. Then Romero, after I nodded to let
him know everything was okay. Romero's English was beginning to improve.
My Spanish had stalled on swearing and beer.

Romero said to me, "Hole?"

In the last joint, I told him the places we stayed were holes. That they were
dives, dumps, death traps, shit shops, fucking slack alleys.

"Yeah, you're right it's a hole," I said.

I stood to unpack and straight away Romero grabs the pillow. Then he folds
it in two and cuddles into it, brings his knees up to his chest and faces the wall.
I almost laughed at the little spic. I guess he must have felt me standing over him
because he turned his head and flashed that cheesy grin. Goes, "Hole. Fucking
hole eh?"

I grabbed his shoulder and pulled him so he was sitting upright.

I goes, "Don't get cute wee man. You know how this works."

He opened his arms wide and shrugged.

"Me no understand. No understand."

He understood.

"Give. Me. The Pillow." And I pointed.

Romero shook his head. "You use," he pulled at my coat. "Me pillow."

"Are you really wanting this argument? Cos I'll burst you. If you get window side then I get pillow. Comprende?"

"No comprende, no comprende," he said.

He lay down again and turned the other way.

I slapped him across the back of his shaved head. Slapped him so hard it stung my hand. But he didn't even turn. He took it. I slapped him again. I pulled my hand away and blew on it. Romero but, he stayed facing that manky window with his knees curled up at his chest.

"Well just suit yourself then," I said. "Have your pillow."

I took my jacket off and rolled it up. I wasn't gonna ask him for a sheet so I ripped one of the curtains from its rail and decided to use that as a cover. It was a hundred fucking degrees but you still like to feel there's something covering you up. I made as much noise as I could during this whole process. I was stomping about and sighing. I kicked off my shoes and they battered off the wall near his head. I lay down and closed my eyes. His breathing was quite fast. He wasn't asleep yet. I lay quietly for a minute or two, then said to him, "Just you sleep with one eye open son. Maybe old Alex here will fuck you up a bit in the night." When I laughed I thought I could hear his muscles tense. I thought his English was getting good.

I woke the next morning with the sun streaming in the window. For the first time since we'd arrived I noticed the stench of the place. Years of dirt had turned the linoleum a muddy brown. It was only in the corners you saw it had been blue once.

"Hey fuck-bucket, wake up!"

Romero stirred and tilted his peanut head over the edge of the bed.

He goes, "Why you sleep floor Alex?"

I had to stop myself from reeling up and biting his nose clean off.

"Why I sleep floor? Why I sleep floor? Why Romero think Alex sleep floor? Is it because A) Alex like floor? B) Alex have nightmare and fall out of bed? Or C) Romero's a gypsy Spic. A gypsy, tea leaf, spic?"

"I think you angry."

"Angry? Oh, Romero thinks he knows emotions now. How about betrayed, disgusted, remorseful, exaspe-fuckin-rated? Do you think I feel those things?"

Romero didn't answer, just stared at me blankly.

I took a deep breath and sat up. Our faces were so close I could smell his breath.

"I'm not angry Romero. I am acting angry but I don't feel angry. The emotion I'm feeling is sadness. Do you know sadness? Sometimes when you feel sad you act angry. Sadness results in anger, do you understand?"

He nodded.

"Repeat after me: 'I feel sad'."

"I feel zad."

"No. Sssss. Enunciate the ssss, fuck sake."

"I feel zzzzad."

"Almost."

I lay back down on the floor. Romero stood up and went to his bag. It was a big rucksack; tatty with hardly any cushioning left on the straps. Depending on how far we'd travelled you'd sometimes see red sores all along the top of his shoulders. He started rifling through it and items began to drop to the floor. Clothes piled up, and old washed out photographs of stupid spics with gypsy clothes and men with handlebar moustaches. He must have been near the bottom of the bag when he found what he was looking for. He brought out two bibles and handed one to me. He left everything else scattered about the room and climbed back into the bed.

"Alex come up," he says.

"I'm fine here man."

He pulled the sheets aside to open up a space for me.

"I says I'm fine."

The pillow he dropped down landed on my face.

"Eh you, watch it."

"Don't feel sad Alex. Come up."

"I'm not sad. I'm angry."

I climbed up into the bed and we lay top to tail. I folded the pillow in two so that I was at an angle where I could read properly. Romero was lying prostrate at his end. I grabbed his calf and shook him.

"Take my jacket and sit up."

He lent down and got it, then sat up, facing me

"Okay. What we reading today then?" I said.

"John."

"You always want to read John. Why you always wanting to read John? Why can't we start at the beginning and just fucking read?"

"John."

"Aye, I've got ears man."

"Chapter fourteen."

I found the page and told Romero the number.

"You start us off," I said.

"No Alex. You read today. I listen."

"You won't learn if I'm always reading."

"Today you read. Later I read."

Romero had his eyes closed and was smiling.

"Do not let your hearts be troubled. Trust in God; trust also in me. In my Father's house are many rooms; if it were not so, I would have told you. I am going there to prepare a place for you. And if I go and prepare a place for you, I will come back and take you to be with me that you also may be where I am. You know the way to the place where I am going."

Romero repeated my words. "The place where I am going," he said.

"Aye. Right, listen. Thomas said to him, 'Lord, we don't know where you are going, so how can we know the way?'"

"They know because he is the way, the truth and the life," Romero said. He was looking at me, nodding.

I shook my head.

"Alex, Alex, stop. I'll read now."

I threw him the English version.

"You're going to have to get used to it."

He looked up at me with those eyes.

I nodded to the English version.

Romero sat up straighter against the wall. He found the place where we'd stopped, coughed and began trying to read. There were some words I knew he didn't know but he knew the whole passage off by heart. Every time he said one of those words though - 'miracles', 'counselor' - he'd look at me and wiggle his eyebrows up and down as if to say see, see, I am a master of the English language. He was reading the Bible and lying at the same time. Then he got to a bit and repeated the same section three times.

"This is my favourite verse," he said. "'I will not leave you as orphans; I will come to you'. He is saying that we will never be alone. That even people like us have someone as long as we believe in God."

"Aye, and you fall for it."

"No. I believe."

"Same thing."

"I believe. When I read that, I know we'll be okay. You will be okay and I will be okay. One day everyone will be orphans."

"Listen man, I am not an orphan. Jesus Christ. And you are not an orphan. We both still have mothers. Your entire definition of what constitutes being an orphan is deluded. See 'cause you speak that fucking pidgin English, maybe that's the problem. But you've got to learn, orphan means no parents. None. Nada. We have parents. A parent. I've got my Mother and you've got yours. "

"But a man without a father is an orphan. A man needs a father. And in God we all have a father."

"Right okay then." I pulled the covers off my chest. "Are we done for today professor?"

"It helps to talk about it Alex."

"Christ. Even here man."

He looked confused.

"I thought we might be removed from that therapy culture shite here. It doesn't make me feel better. So don't tell me talking about it makes me feel better."

"It makes me feel better."

"Well you talk about it then. But don't talk to me. Talk to any old spic you walk past in the street, but don't talk to me."

"Tell me how you feel Alex."

I got up from the bed then and stood over Romero. He lent his head on his palm and looked up at me.

"It gets easier Alex. If you talk about it. Your father wants you to be happy."

"He doesn't want anything."

"He can see you Alex. He looks down upon you."

"I've said don't you start that, okay?" I jabbed my finger in his forehead. "Don't you forget we're reading that book for the English. Nothing else."

Romero knocked my hand away and moved back. He kept his eyes on the book.

"I'm sorry about your father Alex."

Romero went quiet after that. I got down on the floor and did the routine. Twenty press ups, fifty sit ups. Repeat three times. I was out of breath when I stood up and felt my face red with the pressure. Romero was leaning his head on his palm again. I leapt forward, made to slap him and he jumped back.

"What you staring at?" I asked.

"Nothing."

I creaked my neck and felt it crack. He was still looking at me.

I laughed. "What is it man? Is there something you want to say?"

He shook his head and went back to looking at the book. I sat down on the bed opposite him.

"Well read it out loud then, come on. How am I meant to know if you're understanding it or not?"

Romero read quietly. "You heard me say, I am going away and I am coming back to you. If you loved me, you would be glad that I am going to the Father, for the Father is greater than I." He stopped reading and sat staring again.

I wound my hand round to tell him to keep going.

"I have told you now before it happens, so that when it does happen you will believe. I will not speak with you much longer, for the pri... pri..."

"The word's prince. He means the Devil."

Romero didn't look up from the page. He waited until I'd stopped speaking, composed himself, and continued. He spoke louder now, almost shouting, "The prince of this world is coming. He has no hold on me, he has no hold on me, but the world must learn that I love the Father and I do exactly what my Father has commanded me. He has commanded me that I do good in this world, that I will be a healer of men. He has commanded me Alex. It is my Duty. I will make the world better. Because I believe. Maybe if you too believed you could make a difference."

"Finish reading the passage. I believe you should do that."

He took a deep breath, closed the book and looked at me. "I do exactly what my father has commanded me. Come now; let us leave."

"Know that bit off by heart do you?"

Romero nodded.

"Tell me then, what were those last words again Romero, what did that book say? Just so I know you really know your stuff"

He opened to check.

"Tut tut tut. And you call yourself a believer."

"Let us leave, it says."

"Aye? Well let's. It's sunny outside. Let's not waste it. You'll miss the sun when you get to Scotland."

When we left the room the old man who ran the place was saying we'd only paid for one night so we were to get our stuff. He was shouting at me in broken English. I referred him to Romero and walked outside.

We used to get that a lot. Mostly older men. Most of them choosing me to berate as if I was leading Romero astray. Sometimes after Romero had taken over you could hear them shouting all the way down a corridor. The dialect they spoke was different than Romero's and it was only ever when he spoke with them that I realised how quickly he spoke normally. They'd start by shouting at him but he'd say a few things and by the end they'd usually gone quiet. This one didn't make us get our stuff after that. Nor did we have to pay any more money than for the three nights we'd already paid.

Romero came out and patted me on the back. He took the lead and I followed him. He led us in the direction of the town. There was a market and all the spics were rabbling on, making some fucking din. Cars were driving straight through where the market stalls were, keeping their horns pressed down the whole way. Lots of people were slapping the car bonnets and sending them on their way as if it was the most normal thing in the world. Romero led us over to a fountain at the far end of the square. We sat on the edge and drank from a stream of fresh water. I closed my eyes.

"Tell me about Scotland again," he said.

"There's nothing left to tell you."

"Tell me about the Scottish Haggis again."

"Let me enjoy the sun man."

"Come on Alex, please. The Haggis."

I opened my eyes.

"Okay, okay. The Scottish Haggis. Well... It's a tame animal that many keep as a household pet. Similar to a cat or dog in a sense. Or to you lot, a pig. It is well known for being friendly. So friendly in fact that in Scotland it's the Haggis who is known as man's best friend."

Romero grabbed at my arm. "Tell me what it looks like Alex. Tell that."

"You don't want to know that. You had fucking nightmares the last time."

"No. No nightmares. You tell me and I draw it."

Romero got out his pad of paper and one of his black fine tip pens.

"Okay, okay. Well the Haggis is about the size of a large goat but makes a noise not unlike a chicken. Except it's deeper. It has... Do you remember how many eyes it has Romero?"

"Eleven eyes. An eye for every year of its life."

"Aye, that's right. Well remembered. It has eleven eyes and they follow you wherever you go."

Romero's scribbling away. He goes, "What shape are the eyes?"

"All different shapes and sizes. It just depends."

Romero carried on, drawing all these square eyes and circular eyes. Then he drew the spiky hair that I described in detail and the tartan patterned skin that is used to make tartan. The wee fucker, drawing away with his tongue stuck out.

"Aww, perfecto Romero! That looks like my wee pet Haggis that I have in the house. I call him Pepe."

Romero stands up and fires that cheeser at me. "My cousin. He too is Pepe!"

"Is that right? Christ. Small fucking world eh?"

He nodded like a wee boy.

"And now tell me about the women," he said.

"I'm not telling you about the women."

"The women Alex, the women."

"Not the fucking women. Not today."

He dipped his head and went quiet. I got to enjoy the sun for a minute or two. Until he started again.

"Alex," he said, "there is another woman for you. But maybe not here. We should go to Scotland immediate."

"Immediately."

"Yes! Yes we should!"

"No. I mean the word is immediately."

"But we go soon yes?"

"Aye, we'll go soon."

For the rest of the day Romero showed me around town. It was like he'd been before although I knew he hadn't. He just saw each town we went to as a step closer to reaching Scotland. Every now and again we'd stop and he'd point at something; a bar, a post office, an old lady in the street, and he'd say "word?" and I'd try and say the right word. It should have been that I was taking it in, but my thoughts were back in Scotland. Romero's English was getting better by the hour. Maybe he was more determined. Maybe it was 'cause he was younger than me.

We made it to a bar and I went up and ordered. Money had been getting tight but we could always find enough for beer. Romero had a stash somewhere and when I was totally rooked he'd keep the beers rolling in. Romero went away and left me like he always did. In the places we drank, in that place, people tended to stay away from me. The drinkers were men. People looked dirty. Some spat on the floor and the barman didn't care. Romero came back every so often to check on me. I was getting filthy drunk and he was laughing at me.

"Loco," he said.

He pointed at his head, looped his finger and rolled his eyes.

"Crazy!" said I, laughing so hard that some of the men turned and stared at me long after I'd stopped.

I ordered tequila with a beer to wash it down but I had no cash to pay the man. I shouted for Romero. He appeared from the crowd and spoke quickly. From what I could make out there was some disagreement. The man shouted and went to step from behind the bar. Romero turned his back to me and gave the man an extra note.

On the walk home I was singing.

"Policia," said Romero. "They'll lock you up if you're crazy."

"Ahh my brother. They may take our lives but they'll never take our..."

I paused.

"You must be quiet now," he said.

"I said they'll never take our..."

"Alex you must stop now," he said

"Freedom! Our fucking freedom Romero!"

A few lights went on in the houses at either side of the path.

"You will get us put in prison Alex." He grabbed me by the collar and pushed me away. I lost my balance and fell to the ground. The dust clouded up around me and I lay down for a bit looking through it at the stars.

"You're still a free man Romero," I called. "Don't forget that. You've got it all ahead of you, but me? I wasted the best thing I ever had. She's gone forever. What have I got without her?"

He ran to me and knelt down, grabbing me again by the neck. He shouted some shit in Spanish. Said it really fast and his spit covered my face.

"You loco!" I said.

He was hissing at me now. "Stop shouting. Stop shouting. Stop shouting."

I had to phone home. I had to, I just had to. Back at the hostel I wouldn't let it rest. I refused to stop walking along the corridors banging on every fucking papier-mâché door that we passed.

I told Romero, "I am entitled to one phone call. I am entitled to one phone call." He tried to shoosh me but I was sick of his attitude and slapped him across the head. He reared as if he was going to react. I told him to come ahead, but he wouldn't.

It didn't take long for the boss man to come stomping down the stairs and along the corridor from his ivory tower on the top floor. He screamed a lot of pish at me and I spat on the floor by his bare feet. He ran for me. I was ready for him but Romero got in the way and held him back. The man was shouting about policia but Romero walked him up the corridor away from me. People were popping their heads out of the doors and I was shutting the doors back on them. I made out Romero handing the boss man a bunch of notes and clasping his hands as if in prayer. He came down and told me I had my phone call.

The boss man's room was nothing like the shithole we had to stay in. We had linoleum and he had rugs. We had a hole to shit in and shower over. He had a bathroom suite. And a phone. I ran for it and nearly pulled the thing out its socket. I dialled her number and stood up straight. The boss man was in the corner staring at me and Romero was talking softly to him, his hand pressed out flat towards the man.

The phone took a long time to ring. When it did I listened until it seemed like it had always been ringing. The boss man shouted something and I looked up. Romero was blocking the man's eyes from mine. A little later the phone cut itself off. I tried her again and the same thing happened. Eventually I gave up and called my mother instead.

"I'm on my way home," I cried to her. "I can't do this anymore."

When we got into our room I fell onto the bed. Romero hauled my legs up for me and rested my head on the pillow. "Everything will be okay tomorrow," he said. "Soon we'll leave here and you will take me to Scotland." I drifted in and out of sleep for what must have been most of the night. There were stretches where I watched him. He was on the floor kneeling up and reading that Bible. Page after page he went through, devouring the words, his lips moving as his finger skimmed along each line.

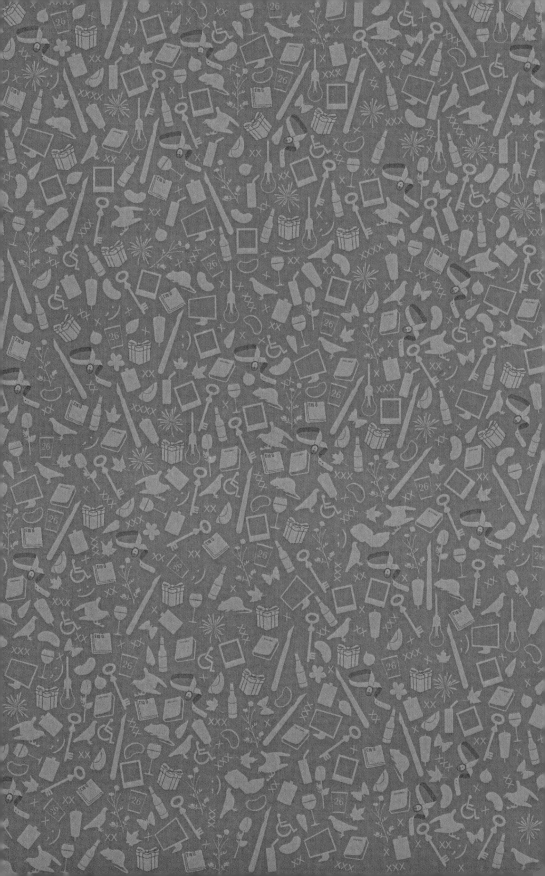

Thanks!

I once read that, "A short story collection is a joint effort." It's true.
This book could not have happened without the help of many people.

Thanks to my Mum, Dad, Robert, Lauren, Robert and Robina (my two families)
for their support and encouragement. Mum, thanks for getting pretty much
everyone you've ever met to support the book. To my brother – thanks for
getting the young team into my stories. DJ Bert K 2k6! Hahaha! To my sister
– are you a girl or something?

To Tricia, Graham, Amanda and Douglas – thanks for being brilliant and mad
and funny and being there the last ten years.

To my friends since school Suthy, Laidlaw, Cockles and Watson – you're all 2625s.
Dave – Biggles – so ruddy, bloody, brave.

To Alan McMunnigall and the Tuesday night class – the stories couldn't have
been written without you. You taught me how to write. These are our stories.
Let's keep searching for the truth.

To everyone at Cargo – I couldn't have asked for a better publisher – enthusiastic,
hardworking and passionate about books. Scotland needs a publisher like you.

To Rodge Glass – Doc, your edits were usually always kind and usually always right
– I really can't thank you enough.

To Mark Buckland – have you put a firework up the arse of Scottish literature yet?

And everyone else – Gran, Grandad, Gradma, Grandpa, Michael, Lynn,
Christopher, Rachael, all my family, the schools, teachers and pupils that have
tolerated me, the writers and literature nights who have helped me improve –
Kirstin and Anneliese for first putting me on at Words Per Minute, Wendy and
Lorna at Monosyllabic, Bissett for the compliments about my hair, Doug Johnstone,
Andrew Raymond Drennan and the other great writers I've read alongside,
thanks for having me. Huge thanks to David Kenvyn at East Dunbartonshire
Libraries – the most shameless and supportive librarian in the land.

And finally, thank you to my beautiful fiancé, Julie Mackay for being an amazing
cover designer, typesetter, supporter and person. You just fit. I love you.

Thanks for reading...

Find out more...

For more stories, information and updates check out the following links:

www.twitter.com/mrallanwilson
www.allanwilsonbooks.com
www.twitter.com/cargopublishing
www.cargopublishing.com

To find out more about who designed this book contact:
julie.mackay@hotmail.co.uk

To enjoy more of Allan Wilson's stories, use these tags:

 Kindle for
Wasted in Love.

 Bonus Edition Book
If it Gets Worse We'll Run.